HE IS COMING FOR YOU

A REBEKKA FRANCK MYSTERY

WILLOW ROSE

BOOKS BY THE AUTHOR

HARRY HUNTER MYSTERY SERIES

- ALL THE GOOD GIRLS
- RUN GIRL RUN
- NO OTHER WAY
- NEVER WALK ALONE

MARY MILLS MYSTERY SERIES

- WHAT HURTS THE MOST
- YOU CAN RUN
- YOU CAN'T HIDE
- CAREFUL LITTLE EYES

EVA RAE THOMAS MYSTERY SERIES

- DON'T LIE TO ME
- WHAT YOU DID
- NEVER EVER
- SAY YOU LOVE ME
- LET ME GO
- IT'S NOT OVER
- TO DIE FOR

EMMA FROST SERIES

- ITSY BITSY SPIDER
- MISS DOLLY HAD A DOLLY
- RUN, RUN AS FAST AS YOU CAN
- CROSS YOUR HEART AND HOPE TO DIE
- PEEK-A-BOO I SEE YOU

- TWEEDLEDUM AND TWEEDLEDEE
- EASY AS ONE, TWO, THREE
- THERE'S NO PLACE LIKE HOME
- SLENDERMAN
- WHERE THE WILD ROSES GROW
- WALTZING MATHILDA
- DRIP DROP DEAD
- BLACK FROST

JACK RYDER SERIES

- HIT THE ROAD JACK
- SLIP OUT THE BACK JACK
- THE HOUSE THAT JACK BUILT
- BLACK JACK
- GIRL NEXT DOOR
- HER FINAL WORD
- DON'T TELL

REBEKKA FRANCK SERIES

- ONE, TWO...HE IS COMING FOR YOU
- THREE, FOUR...BETTER LOCK YOUR DOOR
- FIVE, SIX...GRAB YOUR CRUCIFIX
- SEVEN, EIGHT...GONNA STAY UP LATE
- NINE, TEN...NEVER SLEEP AGAIN
- ELEVEN, TWELVE...DIG AND DELVE
- THIRTEEN, FOURTEEN...LITTLE BOY UNSEEN
- BETTER NOT CRY
- TEN LITTLE GIRLS
- IT ENDS HERE

MYSTERY/THRILLER/HORROR NOVELS

- In One Fell Swoop
- Umbrella Man
- Blackbird Fly
- To Hell in a Handbasket
- Edwina

HORROR SHORT-STORIES

- Mommy Dearest
- The Bird
- Better watch out
- Eenie, Meenie
- Rock-a-Bye Baby
- Nibble, Nibble, Crunch
- Humpty Dumpty
- Chain Letter

PARANORMAL SUSPENSE/ROMANCE NOVELS

- In Cold Blood
- The Surge
- Girl Divided

THE VAMPIRES OF SHADOW HILLS SERIES

- Flesh and Blood
- Blood and Fire
- Fire and Beauty
- Beauty and Beasts
- Beasts and Magic
- Magic and Witchcraft

- WITCHCRAFT AND WAR
- WAR AND ORDER
- ORDER AND CHAOS
- CHAOS AND COURAGE

THE AFTERLIFE SERIES

- BEYOND
- SERENITY
- ENDURANCE
- COURAGEOUS

THE WOLFBOY CHRONICLES

- A GYPSY SONG
- I AM WOLF

DAUGHTERS OF THE JAGUAR

- SAVAGE
- BROKEN

FOREWORD

One, two, He is coming for you.
Three, four, better lock your door.
Five, six, grab your crucifix.
Seven, eight, gonna stay up late.
Nine, ten, you will never sleep again.

PROLOGUE

One, two...the song kept repeating in his head. Sure, he knew where it came from. It was that rhyme from the horror movies. The ones with the serial killer, that Freddy Krueger guy with a burned, disfigured face, red and dark green striped sweater, brown fedora hat, and a glove armed with razors to kill his victims in their dreams and take their souls, which would kill them in the real world. "A Nightmare on Elm Street," that was the movie's name. Yes, he knew its origin. And he had his reasons for singing that particular song in this exact moment. He knew why, and so would his future victims.

He lit a cigarette and stared out the window at a waiting bird in the bare treetop. Waiting for the sunlight to come back, just like the rest of the kingdom of Denmark at this time of the year. Waiting for spring with its explosion of colors, like a sea of promises of sunlight and a warmer wind. But still the winter had to go away. And it hadn't. The trees were still naked, the sky gray as steel, the ground wet and cold. February always seemed the longest month in the little country, though it was the shortest on the calendar. People talked about it every day as they showed up for work or school.

Every freaking day since Christmas.

Now, it wouldn't be long before the light came back. But in reality it always took months of waiting and anticipating before spring finally appeared.

The man staring out the window didn't pay much attention to the weather though. He stood with his cigarette between two fingers. To him, the time he had been waiting ages for was finally here.

He kept humming the same song, the same line. One, two, he is coming for you...The cigarette burned a hole in the parquet floor. He picked up the remains with his hands, wearing white plastic gloves, and carefully placed them in a small plastic bag that he put in his brown briefcase. He would leave no trace of being in the house where the body of another man was soon to be found.

He closed the briefcase and went into the hall, where he sat in a leather chair by the door to the main entrance.

Waiting for his victim to come home.

He glanced at himself in the mirror by the entrance door. He could see from where he was sitting how nicely he had dressed for the occasion.

He was outfitted in a blue blazer with the famous Trolle coat of arms on the chest, a little yellow emblem with a red headless lion—the traditional blazer for a student of Herlufsholm boarding school. The school was located by the Susaa River in Naestved, about eighty kilometers south of Copenhagen, the capital of Denmark. As the oldest boarding school in Denmark, the school took pride in an array of unique traditions. Some of them the world outside never would want to know about.

The blazer was now too small, so he couldn't close it, but otherwise he looked almost like he did back in 1986. He was, after all, still a fairly handsome man. And unlike the majority of the guys from back then, he had kept most of his hair.

His victim had done well for himself, he noticed. No surprise in that, though, with parents who were multibillionaires. The old villa by the sea of Smaalandsfarvandet in the southern part of Zeeland was big and admirable. It could easily fit a couple of families. It was typical of his victim to have a place like this just as his holiday residence.

When he heard the Jaguar on the gravel outside, he took the glove out of the briefcase and put it on his right hand. He stretched his fingers and the metal claws followed.

He listened for voices, but didn't hear any, to his satisfaction.

His victim was alone.

1

"We're going to be too late. Do you want me to be fired on my first day?" I yelled for the third time while gazing up the stairs for my six-year-old daughter, Julie.

"Go easy on her, Rebekka. It's her first day too," argued my father.

He stood in the doorway to the living room of my childhood home, leaning on his cane. I smiled to myself. How I had missed him all these years living in the other part of the country. Now he had gotten old, and I felt like I had missed out on so much and that he had missed out on so much of our lives too. It was fifteen years since I left the town to study journalism. I had only been back a few times since, and then, of course, when Mom died five years ago. Why didn't I visit him more often, especially after he was alone? Instead, I had left it to my sister to take care of him. She lived in Naestved about fifteen minutes away.

Well there was no point in wondering now.

"You can't change the past," my dad would say. And did say when I called him crying my heart out and asking him if Julie and I could come and stay with him for a while.

I sighed and wished I could change the past and change everything about my past. Except for one thing. One delightful little blond thing.

"I'm ready, Mom."

Her.

Julie is the love of my life. Everything I've done has been for her and her future. I sacrificed everything to give her a better life. But that meant I had to leave it all behind—her dad, our friends and neighbors, and my career with a huge salary. All for her.

"I'm ready." She ran down the stairs looking like an angel with her beautiful blond hair braided in the back.

"Yes, you are," I nodded and looked into her bright blue eyes. "Do you have everything ready for school?"

She sighed with annoyance and walked past me.

"Are you coming or not?" she asked when she reached the door.

I picked up my bag from the floor, kissed my dad on the cheek, and followed my daughter, who waited impatiently.

"After you, my dear," I said, as we left the house.

I FOUND a job at a local newspaper in Karrebaeksminde. It wasn't much of a promotion, since I used to work for one of the biggest newspapers in the country. *Jyllandsposten* was located in Aarhus, the second biggest town in Denmark. That was where we used to live.

When I had a family.

I used to be their star reporter, one of those who always got the cover stories. Moving back to my childhood town was not an easy choice, since I knew I had to give up my position as a well-known reporter. But it had to be done. I had to get away.

Now, after dropping off my daughter at her new school and smoking two cigarettes in anxiety for my daughter's first day, I found myself at my new workplace.

"YOU MUST BE REBEKKA FRANCK. Welcome to our editorial room," said a sweet elderly lady sitting at one of the two desks piled high with stacks of paper. I looked around the room and saw no one else. The room was a mess, and so was she. Her long red hair went in all directions. She had tried to tame it with a butterfly hair clip, but it didn't seem to do the job. She got up and waddled her chubby body in a flowered yellow dress over to greet me.

"I'm Sara," she said. "I'm in charge of all the personal pages. You know, the obituaries and such. People come to me if they need to put in an announcement for a reception or a fifty-year anniversary celebration. Stuff like that. That's what I do."

I nodded and looked confused at all the old newspapers in stacks on the floor.

"You probably would like to see your desk."

I nodded again and smiled kindly. "Yes, please."

"It's right over there." Sara pointed at the other desk in the room. Then she looked back at me, smiling widely. "It's just going to be the two of us."

I smiled back, a little scared of the huge possibility of going insane in the near future. I knew it was a small newspaper that covered all of Zeeland, and that this would only be the department taking care of the local news from Karrebaeksminde. But still...two people. Could that be all?

"Do you want to see the rest of your new workplace?" Sara asked and I nodded.

She took a couple of steps to the right and opened a door. "In here we have a small kitchen with a coffeemaker and the bathroom."

"Let me guess. That's it?" I tried not to sound too sarcastic. This was really a step down for me, to put it mildly.

Sara sat down and put on a set of headphones. I moved a stack of newspapers and found my chair underneath. I opened my laptop and up came a picture of Julie, me, and her dad on our trip to Sharm el-Sheikh in Egypt. We all wore goggles and big smiles. Quickly, I closed the lid of the laptop and closed my eyes.

Damn him, I thought. Damn that stupid moron.

I got up from the desk and went into the break room to grab a cup of coffee. I opened the window and lit a cigarette. For several minutes I stared down at the street. A few people rushed by. Otherwise it was a sleepy town compared to where I used to live. I thought about my husband and returning to Aarhus, but that was simply not an option for me. I had to make it here.

I drank the rest of the coffee and killed my cigarette on the bottom of the mug. Then I closed the window and stepped back into the editorial room.

I need to clean this place up, I thought, but then regretted the idea. It was simply too much work for one person for now. Maybe another day. Maybe I could persuade Sara to help me. I looked at her with the gigantic headphones on her ears. It made her face look even fatter. It was too bad that she was so overweight. She actually had a pretty face and attractive brown eyes. She looked at me and took off the headphones.

"What are you listening to?" I asked, and expected that it was a radio station or a CD of her favorite music. But it wasn't.

"It's a police scanner," she said.

I looked at her, surprised. "You have a police scanner?"

She nodded.

"I thought police everywhere in the country had shifted from traditional radio-scanners to using a digital system."

"Maybe in your big city, but down here we still use the old-fashioned ones."

"What do you use it for?"

"It is the best way to keep track of what is happening in this town. I get my best stories to tell my neighbors from this little fellow," she said, while she leaned over gave the radio a friendly tap. "We originally got this baby for journalistic purposes, in order to be there when a story breaks, like a bank has been robbed or something like that. But the past five or six years, nothing much has happened in our town, so it hasn't brought any stories to the newspaper. But I sure have a lot of fun listening to it."

She leaned over her desk with excitement in her brown eyes.

"Like the time when the mayor's wife got caught drunk in her car. That was great. Or when the police were called out to a domestic dispute between the pastor and his wife. As it turned out she had been cheating on him. Now that was awesome."

I stared at the woman in front of me and didn't know exactly what to say. Instead, I just smiled and started walking back to my desk, when she stopped me.

"Ah, yes, I forgot. We are not all alone. We do have a photographer working here too. He only comes in when there's a job for him to do. His name is Sune Johansen. He looks a little weird, but you'll learn to love him. He's from a big city too."

2

Didrik Rosenfeldt thought of a lot of things when he got out of the car and went up the stairs to his summer residence. He thought about the day he just had. The board meeting at his investment company went very well. He fired three thousand people from his windmill company early in the afternoon without even blinking. The hot young secretary gave him a blow job in his office afterwards. He thought about his annoying wife who kept calling him all afternoon. She was having a charity event this upcoming Saturday and kept bothering him with stupid details, as if she would ever be sober enough to go through with it. Didn't she know by now that he was too busy to deal with that kind of stuff? He was humming when he reached the door to the house by the sea.

A tune ran through his head, his favorite song since he was a kid. "Money makes the world go round. A mark, a yen, a buck, or a pound. That clinking clanking sound can make the world go 'round." Didrik sighed and glanced back at his shiny new silver Jaguar. Money did indeed make the world go around. And so did he.

A lot of thoughts flitted through Didrik's head when he put the key in the old hand-carved wooden door and opened it. But death was not one of them.

"You!" was his only word when his eyes met the ones belonging to a guy he remembered from school. A boy, really, as he always thought of him. The boy had the nerve to be sitting in his new leather chair—"The Egg" designed by Arne Jacobsen—and wearing his despicable grubby old blazer from the boarding school. The boy was about to make a complete fool of himself. Didrik shut the door behind him with a bang.

"What do you want"? He placed his briefcase on the floor, took off his long black coat, and hung it on a hanger in the entrance closet. He sighed and looked at the man with pity.

"So?"

ALL THE GIRLS at Herlufsholm boarding school had whispered about the boy when he first arrived there in ninth grade. Unlike most of the rich high-society boys, including Didrik Rosenfeldt, who was both fat and red-headed, the boy was a handsome guy. He had nice brown hair and the most sparkling blue eyes. He was tall and the hard work he used to do at his dad's farm outside of Naestved had made him strong and muscular, and Didrik and his friends soon noticed that the girls liked that...a lot.

The boy wasn't rich like the rest of them. In fact, his parents had no money. But in a strange way, that made him exotic to the girls. The poor countryside boy, the handsome stranger from a different culture who might take them away from their boring rich lives. They thought he could rescue them from ending up like their rich drunk mothers. How his parents were able to afford the extremely expensive school, no one knew. Some said he was there because his mother used to do it with the headmaster, but Didrik knew that wasn't true. This boy's family was—unlike everybody else's at the school—hardworking, earnest people. The kind who people like Didrik had no respect for whatsoever, the kind his father would exploit and then throw away. He and his type were expendable. They were workers. And that made it even more fun to pretend he would be the boy's friend.

Despite that he was younger than they were, they had from time to time accepted him as their equal in the brotherhood.

But, because of his background, he would always fall through. And they would laugh at him behind his back, even sometimes to his face. Like the time when they were skeet shooting on Kragerup Estate, and Didrik put a live cat in the catapult. Boy, they had their fun telling that story for weeks after. How the poor pretty boy had screamed, when he shot the kitty and it fell bleeding to the ground. What a wimp.

"So, what do you want? Can't you even say anything? Are you that afraid of me?" Didrik said arrogantly.

The pretty boy stood up from the seven-thousand-dollar chair and took a step toward him, his right hand hidden behind his back. Didrik sighed again. He was sick and tired of this game. It led nowhere and he was wasting his time. Didrik was longing to get into his living room and get a glass of the fine nine-hundred-dollar cognac he just imported from France. He was not going to let a stupid poor boy from his past get in the way of that. That was for certain. He loosened his tie and looked with aggravation at the boy in front of him.

"How did you even get in here?"

"Smashed a window in the back."

Didrik snorted. Now he would have to go through the trouble to get someone out here to fix it tonight.

"Just tell me what you want, boy."

The pretty blue eyes stared at him.

"You know exactly what I want."

Didrik sighed again. Enough with these games! Until now he had been patient with this guy. But now he was about to feel the real Rosenfeldt anger. The same anger Didrik's dad used to show when Didrik's mother brought him into his study and he would beat Didrik half to death with a fire poker. The same anger that his dad used to show the world that it was the Rosenfeldts who made the decisions. Everybody obeyed their rules because they had the money and the power.

"You're making a fool of yourself. Just get out of here before I call someone to get rid of you. I'm a very powerful man, you know. I can have you killed just by pressing a number on my phone," he said, taking out a black iPhone from his pocket.

"I know very well how powerful you and your family are. But we are far away from your thugs; and I will have killed you by the time they get here."

Didrik put the phone back in his pocket. He now sensed the boy was more serious than he first anticipated.

"Do you want to kill me? Is that it?"

"Yes."

Didrik laughed out loud. It echoed in the hall. The boy did not seem intimidated. That frightened him.

"Don't be ridiculous. You are such a fool. A complete idiot. You always were." Didrik snorted. "Look at you. You look like a homeless person in that old school blazer. Your clothes are all dirty. And when did you last shave? What happened to you?"

"You did. You and your friends. You ruined my life."

Didrik laughed again. This time not nearly as loud and confident.

"Is it that old thing you are still sobbing about?"

"How could I not be?"

"Come on. It happened twenty-five years ago. Christ, I didn't even come up with the idea." Didrik snorted again. "Pah! You wouldn't dare to kill me. Remember, I am a nobleman and you are nothing but a peasant who tried to be one of us for a little while. You can take the boy away from the farm, but you can't take the farm out of the boy. You have always been nothing but a stupid little farmer boy."

Didrik watched the boy lift his right hand, revealing a thing from his past, something he couldn't forget. With a wild expression in his eyes, he then moved the blades of the glove and took two steps in Didrik's direction with them all pointing at him. It scared the shit out of him. It had been years since he last saw the glove and thought it had been lost. But the pretty boy had found it. Now the ball was in the boy's court.

"I can give you money." Desperately, he clung to what normally saved him in troubled times. "Is it money you want? I could call my secretary right now and make a transfer."

He took out the iPhone again.

"I could give you a million. Would that be enough? Two million? You could buy yourself a nice house, maybe get some nice new clothes, and buy a new car."

The boy in front of him finally smiled, showing his beautiful bright teeth. Phew! Money had once again saved him. At least he thought. But only for a second.

"I don't want your blood money."

Didrik didn't understand. Who in the world would say no to money? "But..."

"I told you. I want you dead. I want you to suffer just as I have been for twenty-five years. I want you to be humiliated like I was."

Didrik sighed deeply. "But why now?"

"Because your time has run out."

"I don't understand."

The boy with the pretty blue eyes stepped closer and now stood face to face with Didrik. The four claws on his hand were all pointing towards Didrik's head. The boy's eyes were cold as ice, when he said the words that made everything inside Didrik Rosenfeldt shiver: "The game is over."

3

Lari Soerensen enjoyed her job as a housekeeper for the Rosenfeldt family. Not that she liked Mr. Rosenfeldt in particular, but she liked taking care of his summer residence by the sea. They barely ever used it, only for a few weeks in the summer and whenever Mr. Rosenfeldt had one of his affairs with a local waitress or his secretary. He would escape to the house in Karrebaeksminde for "a little privacy" as he called it.

But otherwise there wasn't much work in keeping the house clean, and Lari Soerensen could do it at her own pace. She would turn on the music in the living room and sing while she polished the parquet floor. She would eat of the big box of chocolate in the kitchen. She would take the money in the ashtrays and the coins lying on the shelves and put it in her pocket, knowing the family would never miss it. Sometimes she would even use the phone to call her mother in the Philippines, which normally was much too expensive for her. Her Danish husband didn't want to pay for her phone calls to her family anymore, and since he took all the money she got from cleaning people's houses, she couldn't pay for the calls herself.

It was a cold but lovely morning as she walked past the port and glanced at all the yachts that would soon be put back in the water when spring arrived. All the rich people would go sailing and drinking on their big boats.

She took in a breath of the fresh morning air. She had three houses to clean today and she would begin with Mr. Rosenfeldt's, since he probably wouldn't be there. It was only five-thirty, and the city had barely awakened. Everything was so quiet, not even a car.

She had taken a lot of time to get used to living in the little kingdom of Denmark. Being from the Philippines, she was used to a warmer climate, and people in her homeland were a lot more open and friendly than what she experienced here. Not that they were not nice to her—they were. But it was hard for her to get accustomed to the fact that people didn't speak to you if they didn't know you. If she talked to a woman in the supermarket, she would answer briefly and without looking at Lari. It wasn't impolite; it was custom. People were busy and had enough in themselves.

But once people got to know somebody, they would be very friendly. They wouldn't necessarily stop and talk if they met in the street. Often they were way too busy for that, but they would smile. And Lari would smile back, feeling accepted in the small community. If people became friends with someone, they might even invite them to dinner and would get very drunk, and then the Danes wouldn't stop talking until it was early in the morning. They would tell a lot of jokes and laugh a lot. They had a strange sense of humor that she had to get used to. They used sarcasm all the time, and she had a hard time figuring out when they actually meant what they said or when they were just joking.

But Lari liked that they laughed so much. She did too. Smiled and laughed. That's how she got by during the day, the month, the year. That's what she did when the rich white man from Denmark came to her house in the Philippines and told her mother, that he wanted to marry Lari and take her back to Denmark and pay the family a lot of money for her. That's what she did when she signed the paperwork and they were declared married, and she knew her future was saved. She smiled when she got on the plane with her ugly white husband, who wore clogs and dirty overalls. She even smiled when he showed her into the small messy house that hadn't been cleaned for ages and told her that was her new home. That her job would be to cook and clean and be available to him at any time. She was still smiling, even at the end of the day when she handed over the money that she earned from housecleaning, while her husband sat at home and was paid by the government to be unemployed. And when Mr. Rosenfeldt grabbed her and took her into his bed and had oral sex with her, she still smiled.

Yes, Lari Soerensen always smiled. And she still did today when she unlocked the door to Mr. Rosenfeldt's summer residence.

But from that moment on, she would smile no more.

4

I awoke feeling like I was lying under a strange comforter in a foreign place in an unknown city. Slowly, my memory came back to me, when I looked at my sleeping daughter in the bed next to me. When I came home from work she told me the first day of school had been a little tough. The teachers were nice, but the other kids in the class didn't want to talk to her and she had spent the day alone and made no new friends. I told her she would be fine, that it would soon be better, but inside I was hurting. This was supposed to be a fresh start for the both of us, a new beginning. I now realized it wouldn't go as smoothly as I had hoped.

My dad had prepared a nice breakfast for us when we came downstairs...coffee, toast, and eggs. Soft boiled for me and scrambled for Julie. We dove into the food.

Before mom died, he wouldn't go near the kitchen, except to eat, but things had changed since then. He's actually gotten pretty good at cooking, I thought, while secretly observing him from the table. Ever since his fall down the stairs last year, he had to use a cane, but he still managed to get around the kitchen and cook for us.

"You know, Dad, with me in the house, you could catch a break every once in a while. I could take care of you and cook for you instead."

He didn't even turn around, but just snorted at me. "I know my way around. You would only mess the place up."

Then he turned around, smiling at Julie and me, and placed a big plate of scrambled eggs on the table in front of us.

I sighed and rubbed my stomach.

"Sorry, Dad, I'm too full. Julie, go get your bag upstairs. We're leaving in five."

Julie made an annoyed sound and rushed up the stairs.

My dad looked at me seriously.

"She misses him, you know," he said, nodding his head in Julie's direction. "Isn't it about time she got to call him, and talk to him?"

I shook my head. I hated that she had told her granddad she missed her father. Since I couldn't leave my job until late in the afternoon, he had suggested he would pick her up every day and they could spend some quality grandpa-granddaughter time together, catching up on all the years they missed of each others' lives. I liked that, but I didn't care much for him meddling in my life.

"I can't have him knowing where we are."

My dad sighed. "You can't hide down here forever. If he wants to find you, he will. Whatever happened to you up there, you have to face it at some point. You can't keep running from it. It will affect your daughter too. No matter what he did, he is, after all, still her dad."

Now it was my turn to sigh. "Just not right now, okay?"

As I got up, Julie came down and dumped her bag on the floor before sitting down again and taking another serving of eggs.

Where she would put it in her skinny little body, I didn't know, but I was glad to see her eat, despite being so nervous about another day alone in the schoolyard with no one to play with.

"She must be growing," my dad said with a big smile. "That's my girl," he said, and winked at her.

I looked at the clock and decided that I too had the time to sit down for another minute. The radio played an old Danish song from my childhood. My dad started humming and tried to spin around with his cane. He almost fell, but avoided it in the last second, and we all laughed. I began to sing along too and Julie rolled her eyes at me, which made me sing even louder. The old cat stopped licking herself and stared at us from the window. She would probably be rolling her eyes too if she could.

IT WAS one of those beautiful mornings, but a freezing cold one too. The sun embraced everybody, promising them that soon it would triumph over the cold wind. Soon it would make the flowers come out of hiding in the ground and with its long warm arms it would make them flourish and bloom. I really enjoyed my drive along the ocean and the sandy beach. The ocean seemed angry.

I had promised headquarters to do a story today, an interview with an Italian artist, Giovanni Marco, who lived on Enoe, a small island close to Karrebaeksminde. It was connected to the mainland by a bridge. The artist had made a series of sculptures that made the public angry because of their vulgarity. The artist himself claimed that it was his way of making a statement, that art cannot be censored. He had displayed the sculptures in the county's art festival, shocking the public and making people nauseous from looking at them.

He was the same artist who once had displayed ten blenders, each with one goldfish in them in a museum of art, waiting to see if anyone in the audience would press the button and kill the fish. He loved to provoke the sleepy Danes and outrage them. At least they then took a position and cared about something. I remembered he said he wanted to wake them from their drowsy sleep walk. I was actually looking forward to this interview with this controversial man on the beautiful island.

GIOVANNI MARCO LIVED in an old wooden beach house that looked like it wouldn't survive if a big storm should hit the beach. Fortunately, big storms are rare in Denmark. We had a big one in 1999 as strong as a category one hurricane. It was still the one people remembered and talked about. It knocked down trees and electric wires. At least one tree hit a moving car and killed the driver inside. That was a tragedy. It could definitely get very windy, but the artist's house would probably stand for another hundred years.

Barefooted, he welcomed me in the driveway with a hug and a kiss on my cheek, which overwhelmed me, since I had not been happy about male physical contact lately. So I'm sure I came off stiff and probably not very friendly toward him.

He was gorgeous and he seemed to know that a little too well. I never liked men who thought too much of themselves, but this one intrigued me anyway, which made me nervous and uncomfortable in his presence.

His blue eyes stared at me while he invited me inside. It's rare for an Italian man to have blue eyes like that, I thought. Maybe he had Scandinavian genes. Maybe that's why he had escaped from sunny Italy to cold Denmark, where the sun would hide all winter. His hair was thick and brown and his skin looked very Italian. But he was tall like a Scandinavian. And muscular. I hated to admit it, but it was attractive.

Inside, I was stunned by the spectacular view from almost every room in the house: views of the raging ocean, of the wild and absorbing sea. I used to dream about living like that. Well, I used to dream about a lot of things, but dreams have a tendency to get broken over the years.

Giovanni, in a tank top and sweatpants, smiled at me and offered me a cup of organic green tea. I am more of a coffee person, but I smiled graciously and accepted. We sat for awhile on his sofa, glancing out over the big ocean.

"So, you have just returned from the big city?" he asked with an irresistible Italian accent. His Danish was good, but not as good as I expected. I had read that he had lived in the country for more than thirty years. "What made you come back?"

News of my return traveled fast in the small community, I knew that, but how it got all the way out here, I didn't know. Overwhelmed by his directness, I shook my head and said, "I missed the silence and the quiet days, I guess." It wasn't too far from the truth. There had been days in the end, when the city got to me, with all its smartass people drinking their coffee "lattes." It used to be just coffee with milk. I didn't get that. But then again, I didn't get sushi either. Even in the center of Karrebaeksminde they had a sushi restaurant now, so maybe it wasn't a big city thing.

"I miss that too when I'm away from here." Giovanni expressed his emotions widely with his arms, the way Italians did. "Especially when I go back to Milan. I get so tired in the head, you know? All those people, so busy, always in a hurry. To do what? What are they doing that is so important?"

"I wouldn't know," I said, knowing that I used to be one of those busy big-city people always rushing off to something. Rushing after a story to put on the cover. Never stopping to feel the ocean breeze or see the flowers popping up in spring. But I wasn't like that anymore. I had changed. Having to go off to cover the war for the newspaper had changed me. Being a mom changed me. But that was all history.

I began my interview with Giovanni Marco and got some pretty good statements, I thought. I began to see the article take shape in my head. But it seemed more like he wanted to talk about me instead. He kept turning the conversation to me and my past. I didn't like to talk about it, so I gently avoided answering. But he kept pressing on, looking me in the eyes, as if he could see right through me. I didn't like that, and he began to annoy me. His constant flirting with me was a little over the top. Luckily, my cell phone started ringing just as he began asking about my husband.

"I better take this," I said.

"Now? In the middle of our conversation? Now, that is what I think is wrong with this world today. All these cell phones always interrupting everything. People using them on the bus, on trains, in the doctor's waiting room, rambling about this and that, and playing games. God forbid they should ever get themselves into a real conversation. They might even risk getting to know someone outside their own little world."

He got up and looked passionately in my eyes, and I couldn't help smiling. He was indeed over the top, but it was sweet.

"Now, tell me, what could be so vital that it cannot wait until we are done?" He thrust his long Italian arms out in the air.

"It might be about my daughter," I said, and got up from the couch.

IT WASN'T ABOUT JULIE. It was Sara from the newspaper. She was almost hyperventilating, trying to catch her breath. She was rambling.

"Take it easy, Sara," I said, while holding a finger in my other ear to better hear her. "Just tell me calmly what is going on."

She took a pause and caught her breath. "A dead body. The police found a dead body. I just heard it on my radio."

"So?"

"Are you kidding me? That's like the biggest story of this century down here."

I didn't get it. Normally when we received news like that at my old newspaper, they just put in a small note on page five, and that was it. If the police thought it was a murder and an investigation took place, we would make a real article about it, but still only place it on page five. And Sara didn't even know if it was considered to be a murder case or not. It was just a dead body. For all I knew, he could have died of a heart attack.

"Don't people die in this place?" I challenged.

In Aarhus, people died every week. With the gangs of immigrants fighting the rockers, people got shot and stabbed all the time. Of course, there would be a story if a dead body was found. But it wasn't like it was one of the big ones.

"He might have fallen drunk or even had a heart attack," I said, trying to close the conversation. "I'll call the police and get something for a small article when I come back, okay?"

"No, no, no. It is not okay at all. I called Sune. He is already on his way down there. You have to be there before anyone else. I got this from the police radio, remember? That means no one else in the country knows anything yet. It is what you would call a solo story."

I liked the ring of that. I might get it on the cover of the morning paper. Not bad on my second day.

"Okay, give me the address."

5

Half an hour later, I arrived at the scene. As I got near the address, I immediately knew this was no heart attack or just a drunken man. Four police cars were parked in front of the same house, two of them called in from Naestved, the biggest city nearby. I recognized a big blue van as one the forensic team from Copenhagen used.

This was big stuff.

The entrance to the house was blocked by crime tape. On the other side of the tape, policemen searched, wearing suits and gloves, writing in their notebooks, marking trace evidence, dusting for fingerprints, and marking shoeprints.

According to the radio report Sara had heard on the scanner, the victim was a white male, forty-six years old. But I already knew that when I got there. I recognized the house and knew that it could only be Didrik Rosenfeldt. The house used to belong to his parents when I was a kid. And Didrik would come down here on summer vacation from boarding school. He was my sister's age, and I remembered them hanging out together one summer. But something happened and she dumped him and never spoke of him again. He was a real asshole as far as I knew. He used to come down here and flirt with almost anything that had a pulse. He spent his time hanging out on his parents' yacht in the port, drinking with his friends from the boarding school, harassing people who were different than they and had less money. A real prick, I would call him. That probably hadn't changed a bit.

I looked around at the small crowd of neighborhood kids who had gathered in front of the house, peeking in. In the middle, a tall skinny guy stood out. He had a green Mohawk and wore a leather band with spikes around his neck, a leather jacket, and had several piercings in his eyebrows, lips, and nose. He wore black make-up on his eyes and lips. He stood out in stark contrast to this crowd of high society upper-class kids. In his hands, he held a camera that never left his eyes, constantly taking a series of pictures. As I got close to him, I noticed that he was missing two of his fingers on his right hand.

"You must be Sune," I said, when I approached him.

He didn't look down at me, just kept on taking pictures non-stop.

"Mmm…"

"I'm Rebekka Franck. Did you see anything yet?"

"Nope."

"Has the body been taken out yet?"

"Nope."

Great, I thought. Then there was a chance we could get a picture of the covered body on the way into the ambulance. That was always a good shot for an article of this kind.

"Don't you think it's weird, since the body was found at six o'clock this morning?" Sune asked me.

Now that he said it, I did. It was three in the afternoon. Weren't they in a hurry to get the body to the lab right away and find the cause of death?

"Yeah, what does that mean?"

"That the body has been hard to get out. Maybe it was lying under something or was tied to something."

I nodded. This guy knew how to use his head. Not many could do that these days without getting hurt.

"Sounds likely."

"It must at least be a messy crime scene, since it has taken them so long. There are a lot of people in there."

I nodded again. This guy had been at a crime scene before. And it probably wasn't here in Karrebaeksminde where he got that kind of experience.

"You're not from around here, are you?" I asked.

"Nope."

"Copenhagen?"

"Christiania. Have been and always will be a Christianite."

Ah, a free spirit from Christiania. Also known as "fristaden," the free-state. It was an area in Copenhagen that had around a thousand inhabitants. They lived by what they liked to call a collectivistic anarchy. Some called it a socialist anarchy. It meant that everybody living there got to take part in all the decisions. To the Christianites, as they called themselves, it meant they were different from the rest of the society and that they lived by their own rules. To the rest of the world, it meant that this was a place you could go and buy pot on the streets of Christiania, where they sold it out in the open, even though it was illegal in the rest of the country. They were a state within the state that the police didn't touch. They even had their own flag, red with three yellow dots. Today things had changed, though. The liberal government had sent in the police and tried to fight the illegal drug trade, and they wanted to remove all the houses that the Christianites had built themselves.

My guess was that Sune wasn't too thrilled about the police in general. I guessed right.

I KEPT a close eye on the activities behind the crime-scene tape and soon I spotted the detective who seemed to be in charge. He came out of the house and headed towards one of the police cars, and I yelled at him.

"Excuse me. Rebekka Franck, reporter at *Zeeland Times*."

He stopped and stared at me. He then approached.

"Rebekka Franck?"

"Yes."

Surprisingly, he smiled at me.

"You don't remember me?"

I really didn't, but I wouldn't disappoint him. Besides, I really needed his comment for my article.

"Well, of course I do," I lied.

"Michael Oestergaard. You used to take dancing lessons at my aunt's dance studio. Jazz ballet."

"Miss Lejrskov's class. Michael. Oh, yes, I do remember."

I really still didn't, but I remembered my dance teacher. Michael looked to be at least eight or nine years older than me. How could I have remembered him?

"Exactly. I used to hang out there with my brother and look at all the pretty girls. So you're a big-shot reporter now? I must admit, I have been following your career. It has taken you around the world?"

"Sort of."

"And now it has brought you to Karrebaeksminde. I heard from old Miss Jensen in the tourist-information-desk down on Gl. Brovej that you had come back."

"And she was right."

That woman did a little more than informing the tourists around here.

"So you work for the newspaper down here now?"

"Yes, I do."

"And you probably want a comment for your article?"

"I would love that." I was stunned. I couldn't believe his courtesy. Normally, I wouldn't get a single word out of the police until they had a press conference, and then I would only get what all the other reporters got.

"Well, I can't say much." He lowered his voice and got closer. "But it ain't pretty, I can tell you that."

"But, what can you tell me about what happened here? Is it a murder?"

"No doubt about it. Someone broke in through the back door and killed the guy."

"Do you have any suspects?"

"No, but we might begin with his wife," he laughed. "He wasn't exactly known as one of God's better children, if you know what I mean."

"I don't, I'm sorry. So you will be questioning the wife in the near future?"

"Sure, but don't write that. That would be interfering with investigative information. You know that."

"Then please just tell me what I can write."

"Write that the victim has been identified as Didrik Rosenfeldt, CEO and owner of the world-known company Seabas Windmills, and known as a part of the famous and very wealthy Rosenfeldt family. He apparently was killed by an intruder in his summer residence; there is an ongoing investigation, and that...is it, I think."

I wrote everything he said in my notebook.

"Why hasn't the body been removed from the house yet?" I asked.

The detective sighed deeply.

"I really can't get into that."

Sune had probably been right.

"How did he die?"

The detective got an occupied look on his face.

"We don't know yet. That's for the crime lab to figure out. I am sorry, but I really have to get on with my job..."

"But surely you must have an idea?"

"We do, but we won't share it with the public, yet."

I nodded. That's what I expected. The crime scene must have been messy, just as Sune said. I spotted Sune out of the corner of my eye. He took pictures of the body as it was finally removed from the house in a body bag and transported in an ambulance.

"Who found the body?" I asked Detective Oestergaard.

"The housekeeper found him this morning, when she came to clean the house."

"At what time?"

"She called us at six."

"Can we talk to her?"

"Well, I guess I can ask her."

I had to pinch my arm. I'd never met this kind of cooperation from the police. Were they always like this or was it because he knew me? Anyway, he left me for a second and came back with a small Philippine woman with an empty look in her eyes and an expression like she had seen the devil himself and lived to tell about it. It seemed she was still in shock and I knew I had to be careful.

I greeted her with a handshake and introduced myself. The detective left us, his duty calling. I waved at Sune and signaled I wanted him to come and take her picture. He came right away.

"So, that must have been real horrible for you," I began.

"I...I just walked in, like I normally do. Normally, he isn't in the house. I didn't expect...I mean, how could I know?"

"Of course you didn't know. Can you tell me a little about what you saw?"

She didn't look at me, but stared into open air.

"He was dead. Blood everywhere. On all the floors in the living room. All over the parquet. It was like a slaughterhouse. He was shredded to pieces. Ripped apart like an animal would kill its prey. No man could have done this. Only a demon."

6

"Did you write this article about my father?"

The chubby redheaded man in front of me looked like his father back in the days when I used to see him down at the port, hanging out and drinking with his boarding school buddies.

He had been waiting for me at the entrance when I arrived at the newspaper the very next morning. He held the paper with a picture of Didrik Rosenfeldt on the front page.

"Yes, I did." I opened the door into the editorial room.

Didrik Rosenfeldt Jr. followed me all the way to my desk.

"Can I help you, sir?" Sara said, as she came out of the kitchen bearing a cup of coffee and a piece of cake on a plate.

"I want an apology from the newspaper. A formal one."

I looked at him. "For what?"

"For publishing this," he said, and pointed at the interview with the housekeeper. "This line, where she says that a demon killed my father. Giving all kinds of details that the public shouldn't know about. I don't want you to write any more about this case. Do you understand?"

Sara placed a cup of coffee in front of me, and I took it.

"Did you want one too?" I asked.

He snorted and pointed at me with a shaky finger.

"Do you know who I am, and what my family is capable of?"

"I think I might have an idea."

"I warn you..."

"Or what?"

"Or..."

I put down my coffee cup and leaned toward him. I wasn't afraid of anybody, least of all of him.

"Listen. You don't scare me one bit, mister. I have faced a lot worse bastards in my time in Iraq. And by the way, last time I checked, we have freedom of speech in this country. Besides, they were the house-keeper's words, not mine. I just printed them. That is not illegal. So just fuck off."

I hadn't noticed Sune, who had come in the room. Now I saw him smiling for the first time.

Didrik Rosenfeldt Jr. snorted again, very loudly this time, but soon realized that he was defeated. Blushing, he turned around and walked quickly towards the door. Before he left, he turned around and looked at me.

"This is not the last word in this case." He disappeared out of the room. I shook my head and sat down, starting my computer.

"What a prick. Just like his father," I mumbled.

The two others in the room kept staring at me. Sara sat down and Sune started clapping.

"Way to go, Rebekka."

"It was nothing."

"Nothing? You just told the owner of the newspaper to fuck off."

I looked up. "He's the owner of the newspaper?"

"Well, not directly. But his family owns the corporation that owns the newspaper."

I felt my body getting heavier in the seat. "So he could have me fired for doing that?"

Sune sat down at the corner of my table. "He probably wouldn't, I guess."

Sune looked at Sara.

"You'll be just fine," she said, not too reassuringly.

MOVING THROUGH THE DAY, I wanted to write a follow-up article about the murder. I couldn't stop wondering about the case. And I didn't want to. Now that I had risked my job and was probably going to get fired anyway, it didn't matter if I upset Didrik Rosenfeldt's son any more. I wanted to figure this case out.

A man like Didrik Rosenfeldt probably had a lot of enemies who wanted him dead. It could be for financial reasons. He was good for over $6.2 billion. That was 6.2 billion reasons to kill him right there. But he was also about to fire three thousand people in his company. That could have ticked someone off. He also had an investment company that may have made a bad investment for someone. Maybe he cheated someone out of a lot of money.

And then there was the wife angle. He was known around town to be having affairs with a lot of women and taking them to the summer residence. Maybe his wife simply had enough and she wanted him to suffer, to die a merciless death as revenge for humiliating her.

It had been seen before, but mostly in foreign countries. Denmark was a small country with only 5.5 million inhabitants. We didn't have that many killings, or even that much crime compared with many other European countries. And almost every murder case was solved. Ninety-six percent of the cases, to be exact, according to the police department's own records.

I was very intrigued—and somewhat disgusted—by what the housekeeper said about the crime scene and how the body looked when she arrived, and I wanted to know more. Maybe there was something in the way he died or in the way they found him that could tell me what kind of killer we were talking about. Could it have been a sex game that went wrong?

I picked up the phone and called my detective dance school friend at the police station, who was thrilled to hear from me, but he was of no help. They still hadn't gotten the autopsy report yet, so they didn't know exactly what had killed him.

Surprisingly, he ended the conversation by asking me out.

"Like a date?" I asked loudly.

Apparently, it was so loud that Sara looked surprised at me with her headphones on. I smiled and pretended it was nothing, so Sara wouldn't spread the word. She was information central around here. No doubt about that. And I had to be very careful what I let her know about me if I didn't want the rest of the town to know it a few minutes later.

"I'm sorry, Michael. But I just got away from a bad marriage, and I need time to get back on my feet. And my daughter needs stability for now. But thanks. I'm flattered that you would ask."

"But maybe another time then?" He sounded so disappointed.

"Maybe. Let's wait and see." I said goodbye and put the phone down.

So they didn't even know what killed the guy yet. Nothing new to put in the paper then.

I was beginning to get irritated and frustrated, when I suddenly thought about my sister in Naestved. She used to date Didrik, and she and her friends hung out with him. I remembered how they hated him for not treating women well. My sister especially seemed to be angry with him after she dumped him. And it was more than just a normal hurt and anger after a breakup. She loathed him. Detested everything about him and his friends. Maybe I could make a sort of portrait of him.

I called headquarters and they loved the idea. So they hadn't spoken to Junior yet. Fine by me. I would continue. Go out with a bang. Didrik Rosenfeldt was a respected businessman and well known in the jet-set society; he came from a noble family...one of the few left. He was one step from royalty.

But he was also a prick, and I was going to tell the world the truth about him.

7

Henrik Holch gave his credit card to the caterer. He had brought in the staff of the world famous Noma restaurant to cater the party. Everyone knew they had just won the world's best restaurant award last year. It had cost him a small fortune, but since he had a big one, he hardly blinked when they gave him the bill.

"Just charge it to this card."

Long after they all were gone, he could still taste the oysters and reindeer tongue with Jerusalem artichoke and marjoram along with the 2007 Chataeuneuf-Du-Pape "Les Vielles Vignes" from Domaine de Villeneuve Rhone-sud.

As always, his party had been a huge success. Now he needed some time alone, doing what he liked to do.

He crossed the living room, noticing the remains of the party everywhere. His housekeeper would take care of that in the morning, before his kids came for the weekend. Not that he particularly enjoyed their company. They had become annoying over the years, just like their mother. He laughed to himself as he opened a bottle of whiskey and poured himself a large glass.

For now, he preferred to be alone, without the fear that anyone might interrupt him and find out what he was doing. Some things were to be kept to one's self, like his father said once, when he walked in on Henrik masturbating in his room.

In order to get rid of the stench of cigars, he opened the big French doors that led out to the garden. Outside, his landscaper had made a beautiful play of lights for the guests to enjoy when they gazed out the windows. It was indeed beautiful. He unbuttoned his white shirt under the Armani tuxedo and took a deep breath of the cold fresh February air. Everything around him was proof of his success and power. Yes, he had been somewhat of a party boy who wouldn't grow up, as his soon-to-be ex-wife called him. But so what? He deserved it. Yes, he liked to do a little cocaine every once in a while, and, yes, he often had a few strippers attend his parties and he had sex with them afterwards.

So what?

He had always been like that. A real party boy. She knew that when she married him.

So what if he had turned forty-six and still just played around? His wife's parents invented the shoes sold all over the world, and naturally he became the CEO of DECCO shoes when he was done with business school. Not that he ever spent as much time working as he did golfing, yachting, and taking trips to Thailand. But wasn't life supposed to be lived? Who knew when it would be over?

Henrik closed the French doors, went back into the living room, took the remote control, and pushed a button. Then he turned off the lights with another remote. He was alone, finally. It was time for him to dedicate himself to his real pleasure.

Of course he did enjoy the company of all the Danish actors and models, and even occasionally the royal prince and his adorable wife. But to him they were all just faces and words to be forgotten. He wasn't a handsome man by nature, but with a little plastic surgery over the years he had become quite attractive. With the fortune he was set to inherit, he had no problems getting women and sex whenever he wanted it.

But to Henrik, sex with a woman was strictly for the stupid. He enjoyed it, yes, very much, but it wasn't exactly a pleasure the way his trips to Thailand gave him pleasure. The way his movies gave him pleasure.

He opened the locked drawer and took out a DVD. He put it in the player and leaned back on the sofa. No, he certainly didn't know who those kids in the movies were. How could he? Or how they ended up doing what they did to each other and the adults in the movies. How should he know? Why should he care? People did all sorts of things for money. They even killed for money. Why shouldn't they be willing to have sex for money? All Henrik knew was that he paid a gigantic amount of money for it.

The Asian kid in the movie was giving an adult man a blow job and Henrik was just about to reach into his pants, dreaming that it was himself getting taken care of by the sweet children in Thailand, when he felt a violent blow to his head and, instead of pure sexual pleasure, felt nothing but pain in a sea of stars.

8

The song. The song. He knew it, Henrik Holch thought to himself, halfway dreaming, and halfway getting back to reality. There it was again. He couldn't escape it. It sent chills down his spine.

"Three, four, better lock your door," someone hummed. Who was it? And why was it so hard for him to focus? He tried to move his arms, but he couldn't. He squinted to regain his focus and see the figure standing in front of him, humming away. What was this? Why did his head hurt so badly? Finally, he succeeded in opening his eyes and focusing, just to discover that he couldn't move. He was tied to a chair in the middle of his own living room. Tape covered his mouth.

In front of him, a man sat in a chair, staring at him in silence. A brown briefcase sat on his lap. They stayed like that for what seemed like an eternity. He didn't recognize the man at first, but little by little, memories came back to him. Some even overwhelmed him and brought tears to his eyes. Memories that had been blocked out of his brain by the alcohol and cocaine over the years. Memories that he was so certain he had escaped and would never have to deal with again.

It gave him the chills to discover that he was wrong. Boy, was he wrong.

He wanted to ask what he wanted from him. Henrik wanted to

offer him money to leave him alone and not bring up the past. Some things are better kept to yourself, he thought. There is no need to bring back that old story now. Why now? But he still couldn't talk and the man in front of him had decided not to.

The man continued to look at him in silence, and all Henrik could do was groan and moan. Moan over the past and all its cruelty. Moan over the future he was afraid he would never get.

And the man let him do it. He even looked like he was enjoying it.

Was that the purpose of all this? To make him moan? To make him regret everything and ask for forgiveness? If it was, he would do that in an instant. He would crawl on his knees and plead for mercy if it was necessary. And it would be sincere. Heartfelt. Because, the fact was, he really truly did feel badly about what they did back then. And he understood why he was about to pay for it.

Finally, the man in front of him spoke. The sound of his voice again after all these years felt like needles ripping through his flesh.

"Hello, Henrik."

Henrik groaned behind the tape.

"Don't try to speak, because I won't understand a word anyway. And, not to be rude, but I don't give a shit about what you have to say."

The man now opened the briefcase and took something out. Henrik's eyes grew wide. He tried to twist himself in the chair and get free from the wire holding him down. But he had no luck. The man in front of him smiled while he put on the glove. Then he got up and went behind him. Henrik hyperventilated through his nose, while he tried to wring himself out of the chair.

"Nice house you've got here," he said and laid his hands on Henrik's shoulders. The four claws lay gently on the right one. Carefully, he caressed his cheek with one of the claws.

"And you were just about to watch a movie when I disturbed you?" he said, and looked at the big flat-screen on the wall, where he had paused the movie on a close up of the Asian boy with his lips closed around an old white man's dick. The boy's brown eyes were open and looked frightened.

The man put his lips close to Henrik's ears.

"You just got to the good part. I paused it so you wouldn't miss anything while you were out cold." He paused and stared at the screen.

"So that is still what you like. The younger the better, right? Isn't that so? And you have taken it even further than you did back then. They've gotten even younger. How old do you think this boy is? Six? Seven?"

Henrik didn't make a move or even a sound.

"You like that frightened look in his eyes, don't you? That's what turns you on, right? That's what used to turn you on back in school. The fear painted all over their faces. And you were about to have some fun with yourself," he said, and stepped around Henrik and now stood in front of him, looking down at his crotch.

Henrik Holch looked down too and saw that his pants were still open.

The man reached down and took out his dick with his claws. Henrik Holch shuddered.

"See, now you have that look in your eyes. That same look the little boy has," the man laughed. Then he leaned over and put his face next to Henrik's ear.

"Game over."

After that, there was nothing left but Henrik's hysterical moaning and a muffled scream of pain from behind the tape.

9

She was so mad at him, she had not slept all night. All she could think about were the things she wanted to tell her husband when she got ahold of him. Once again, he had let them down, and both kids were crying and didn't want to go to their dad's house for the weekend. It had become a habit of his to disappoint them and forget about them.

The night before, they had a family party at the school. They were supposed to go, all four of them, as a family. As one unit. For the kids' sake. They weren't getting a divorce, she had told them. They were just living apart until they got their problems solved. That was the plan. They had gone to counseling together. Just the two of them and once with the kids. They were trying. At least the three of them were. It seemed Henrik wasn't doing anything to solve this. Again and again, he let them down. He forgot to pick the kids up, he forgot all their appointments, and sometimes he would disappear for two or three days and she couldn't get ahold of him. But she knew where he was. He was in the house or at the golf club, getting drunk and high and not answering the phone. And now she had found out that he had thrown a big party last night, when he was supposed to go to a family event at the kids' school. She had waited for him for two hours and then just taken the kids by herself. She had made excuses for him in front of the other parents.

"Henrik is just so busy lately with the company moving the factory to China and all. You know what it's like." She had laughed gently and the other women laughed back.

All the big-shot husbands were busy and put business before their families. That's just the way it is, they had all agreed.

She refused to give him the divorce he wanted. It wasn't acceptable in her family. They would work things out, or get separate bedrooms in the house and maybe they could be like her own parents, who just stopped talking and lived their separate lives. As long as they showed up to the right parties and charity events and looked like a successful married couple who everybody envied, they were fine, and could do whatever they wanted once they were inside their own house again. Christ, their mansion was big enough for both of them to live there without ever having to have anything to do with each other again. They just didn't get a divorce.

"Not in our family," her mother had said, when she had cried her heart out in front of her and told her about her husband's increasing abuse of drugs and alcohol and the many trips to Thailand and strange videos he would sneak down to watch in the living room when he thought they were all sleeping.

"Learn to live with it; that's what we women do," her mother had snorted and made it very clear that this was not something she was to bring up again. She was supposed to deal with it.

Then she had begun to threaten him. The company he worked for belonged to her family. He would lose everything if they got a divorce. She would get the house, the kids—everything. But it didn't seem to frighten him one bit. He wanted out, he said. He wanted to go away for good. Move permanently to Thailand.

"To do what?" she had yelled desperately. "So you can pay young boys to give you pleasure all day? That's not love, Henrik. That's disgusting."

But he said he didn't care what she thought of him.

"I just want out of this marriage," he said.

But he was not going to get off that easily, she thought, as she reached the driveway of her old home. The yard looked nice. The landscaper had done a nice job. She would remember to give him an extra bonus this month.

It was only six-thirty in the morning and she knew that it was time to take out the trash. She was going to put him in rehab. First she would take away his drinking habit, and then she would find some way to remove the other addiction that was destroying their life. She opened the front door with her key. The smell of cigars and strong alcohol hit her in the face. By the mess in the hall, she could tell that a lot of people had been there...probably models and actors, as usual. Getting high, acting out, having sex in the bedrooms.

"Henrik?" she said out loud.

He was probably passed out in the living room as usual, she thought, and wondered how she would get his sorry ass out to the car. Maybe it wouldn't be too bad if he was passed out. Then he wouldn't be able to resist. She could just drag him out there. But she did bring her gun in her purse. Just in case. That would make him go willingly if he was awake. Or she could threaten to call the police on him. What-ever did the trick.

She never finished the thought, but froze in a scream when she saw the huge puddle of blood.

10

I spent a couple of days researching the story, "Didrik Rosenfeldt's Hidden Past Exposed." With a little help from my sister, I had found out he and a couple of his friends were arrested in 1985, accused of having raped a local girl. My chances of finding the girl were slim. But Sune, our photographer, stepped in. He told me he might be able to find the girl. He used to do "stuff like that." I told him to knock himself out and let him use my computer. It didn't take him long to find the girl's name and discover that she had gotten married and now had a new name, that she lived in Holme-Olstrup, not very far from Karrebaeksminde.

The drive would only take eighteen minutes. I took Sune with me.

"So how did you know how to find her?"

He shrugged. "I just know a little about computers. I do stuff. Or I used to."

"Like a hacker?"

"You might call it that."

"Is that why you went to juvenile prison?"

He looked at me, surprised.

"Well, I know a trick or two," I said. "Journalists can do things with a computer too. Like look people up and check their background. Or find somebody in the police who can."

Sune nodded. "Well, it isn't like it's a secret. But, yes, I used to hack myself into a lot of government stuff and one day I got arrested."

"How old were you?"

"Sixteen."

"So what happened?"

"I did my time. And when I got out I couldn't get a job anywhere. I made some bad friendships that weren't doing me any good. So I thought I had two choices. Either I stayed in Copenhagen and got into even more trouble with the law and became a real criminal or I get the hell out of there."

"And now you're supposed to stay away from hacking, right?"

He nodded. "They'll never know I used your computer to find that girl's name."

"But you hacked into the police database, right? And found the file from back then?"

"Yeah."

"So now I could get in trouble?"

"You won't."

I looked at him. He smiled.

"You have got a lot of confidence, don't you?" I said.

"Well, I am good. I don't leave a trace."

"Good. So why did you get caught when you were sixteen?"

"I was young and not careful. I know better now."

"So what happened to your fingers?" I asked, and looked at his hand where he was missing the two fingers in the middle.

"Juvenile detention." He stared out the window. "I don't want to talk about it."

We had a long pause and reached the city limit of Holme-Olstrup.

"So, you never told me. What are you doing down here in the middle of nowhere?" Sune said, when I had parked the car.

I looked at him and opened my door. "The same as you are, I guess. Hiding from my past."

. . .

45

HOLME-OLSTRUP IS a town mostly known for its amusement park called Bonbon-land. It was started when a man named Michael Spangsberg, who was a candy maker, got the idea for candy with funny names: seagull droppings, dog farts, and pee diapers. The candy became so popular that many schools came to visit the factory located in Holme-Olstrup to see how the candy was made. But because of the hygiene requirements, the factory couldn't have visitors, so the founder decided to open a park, with a candy shop, a movie theater, and four boats in a pond. Today, that had grown into one of the most visited parks in the country, with more than sixty roller coasters and other attractions. It had put the city of Holme-Olstrup on the map.

I had been there once with Julie and her dad, when she was younger, and we were visiting my parents. I remembered the day and felt a little pinch in my heart. We used to be so good together. Better than all the others. We used to care for each other. Now he had ruined everything. How could I have been so blind? Love is blind, my dad would say. It was so true.

IRENE HANSEN OPENED THE DOOR. She was small and skinny with dyed blond hair. When I saw her face, I remembered her from back then. I just never knew her name. Her parents owned the shop at the port in Karrebaeksminde. We used to buy beer and cigarettes at their store on Friday nights when we were hanging out at the port doing nothing but meeting up with boys. She was my sister's age, about ten years older than me. I remembered her as a wild girl, always flirting with the boys, talking dirty, smoking, and drinking. My sister told me the rape had changed her. After that, her parents had been overly protective and never let her go out at night. They accused her of being promiscuous and said it was her own fault the boys raped her. If she hadn't been flirting, it wouldn't have happened; if she didn't dress like a whore, they wouldn't have done it. They had then dropped the charges against Didrik Rosenfeldt and his friends, but that only made everybody think the parents must have been right. She was to blame. Maybe she even led them on, and just regretted it afterwards when she faced the consequences. She got pregnant and had to have an abortion. My sister was one of the only people in the whole town who believed her story.

"Why?" I asked her.

"Because he tried to do the same to me," my sister said.

"What happened?"

"I went with him and his friends on his parents' boat one evening when we were still dating, and he..." she sighed before she continued. "He and his friends from boarding school tried to rape me."

"Why have you never told me?"

"You were just a kid. I've tried to forget it ever since."

"How did you escape?"

"I jumped off the boat in time to get away. It was summer, so the water was warm, and we weren't far from the coast, so I managed to swim all the way to the beach."

"Did you report it?"

"No."

That didn't seem like something my sister would do.

"Why not?" I asked.

"Dad convinced me that it would only mean trouble for the family."

I was so confused. That didn't seem like something dad would say. What had happened to him?

"Why?"

She sighed again.

"I don't know why. Please, just forget about it, okay? There is no reason to be digging in the past now."

WHEN IRENE OPENED THE DOOR, I saw a different girl than the one I remembered. This one was shy and timid. She looked at us with surprise. Normally, I would have called first, but since this was a delicate matter, I wanted to look her in the eyes when I asked her if she would give the interview for the article. I wanted her to see who I was and that I didn't mean to cause her any harm. I just wanted people to know the truth. That's what I told her, and she just stared at me in disbelief and shook her head.

"I don't want to talk about it," she said. "I'm sorry." She was about to close the door when I stopped her.

"Listen, Irene, I know this must be hard for you. But the guy is dead. Murdered. And a lot of people think the world of him...that he was a big-shot businessman. And of course it is a tragedy that he was killed, but I want to tell the world what kind of man he really was."

"I'm sorry, but..."

"You can be anonymous, if you want. No one has to know that it was you."

She looked at me with mistrust.

"There's a lot you don't know about these kinds of people. They will know and come after me. Someone will."

"Please. Just let me hear your side of the story. Or Didrik Rosenfeldt will take it to the grave and you will never have your name cleared. Don't you want that?"

Irene was silent for a long time, and I could sense she was debating within herself. Her mind was a battlefield right now, and I just hoped the right side would win.

After a few more seconds, she stepped back into the house, opened the door, and let us in. I smiled at Sune, who smiled back.

IRENE OFFERED US COFFEE, and we accepted. Sune was really polite and gave her a lot of nice compliments on the house and the décor. It wasn't something I would have thought he knew anything about, but sometimes people just surprise you. And it was helpful. Getting to talk about something that interested her, she relaxed and got comfortable. Sune took some discreet pictures of her for the article, from the back and looking out the window. And by the time we got to the interview, she seemed ready to talk. We all sat down.

"Tell me how it happened. How did you get to know Didrik Rosenfeldt?"

She sighed, preparing herself for the emotions and memories about to flush out of her like a big ocean wave.

"I had known Didrik and his friends from the boarding school for a long time. In the summertime, when their school was closed, they always came down to Karrebaeksminde to stay at Didrik's house on the water or go sailing in his parents' boat. His parents were never there anyway and he and his friends were free to do what they wanted. And so they did."

"So they came in your parents' store at the port?"

"Yes, every time they went out on the boat, which was most days during the summer. They had to get supplies. Mostly cold beers and chips and stuff. So they came to my father's store and that's where I met them. Didrik always spoke so nice to me, acted like a real gentleman. He knew how to talk to women. But he had his appearance against him, you know, he was a little chubby and ugly. So no one ever wanted to be with him. But I thought he was nice and had money, and that attracted me."

"But the other boys had a lot of girls, I bet."

"Oh, yes. The boys always had girls with them out on the boat. And I always stared at them, jealous as I was. I remember that I really wanted to be one of the girls going with them out on the ocean, drinking, partying, and having a good time. I wanted to be one of the chosen ones. But I didn't come from a rich background like they did. I didn't go to boarding school, so I thought they would never take me."

"But they did?"

"Yes. One day. I was always flirting with Didrik because I knew he was the one making the decisions of who would go and who would not. Girls never really wanted to be his girlfriend. They would always choose one of the other boys. And that bothered him. So I chose him to be my ticket to have fun on the water. And one day, when they came into the shop to buy their beers, he asked me politely if I wanted to go with them and eat dinner on the boat and watch the sunset. I would be the only girl aboard. But that was meant as a compliment to me, he said. Because if they brought any other girl, she would be jealous of my beauty. I was thrilled. The one and only. I was to be treated like a queen and I could choose to kiss whoever I wanted of the rich boys."

Irene sighed deeply.

"I was so young and stupid."

"So what happened?"

"I got on the boat and the guys were so nice to me, like real gentlemen. I remember wearing a white summer dress and the wind was warm, unlike a normal Danish summer breeze. I was hot and we all cooled down with cold beers all afternoon. Admittedly, I got a little dizzy from the beer and the heat. By dinnertime I was a little drunk, but not so much that I didn't know what I was doing. So I turned up the music and started dancing. The boys ate steaks and fish fillets they had brought from a restaurant on the port. We had champagne and real Russian caviar, and I felt like I was in heaven, and then I just started dancing. The boys watched me and I closed my eyes for a second, enjoying the moment. When I opened my eyes, I saw an expression on Didrik's face I had never seen before in any man. In any human being. He was like an animal getting ready to eat its prey. His nostrils were distended, and he breathed heavily. His eyes were filled with lust. And he was not the only one looking at me like that. All six boys were staring at me with that same look. The sun had begun to set, and the hunting was about to begin."

Irene shook her head and had tears in her eyes. I reached out and held her hand for awhile. I waited for her to be ready to speak again. I really didn't want to pressure her. After a few minutes, she was ready again. I took a deep breath, sensing that what was about to come would be very unpleasant. And I was right.

"They closed in on me. They got up and walked slowly towards me, smiling. I asked them if they wanted to dance, and they laughed. 'It's time to dance, all right,' one said, and grabbed my wrist in an iron fist. It hurt. 'We'll do the leading,' he whispered in my ear. I was scared and tried to pull away, but he held me tightly, and I suddenly felt a hand under my dress. Someone ripped off my panties and I started crying, pleading with them to let me go. Then they threw me to the deck of the yacht and took off my dress. They held my arms and legs. They were laughing and singing."

"What did they sing?"

She started humming. "That song from the horror movies popular back in the eighties. The one with the guy who had knives on his hands," she said.

"Freddy Krueger?" I remembered the movies. There were a lot of them, as far as I knew. I wasn't allowed to watch them until I was older, and by then they weren't that interesting anymore. But I remembered my sister talking about them and teasing me, telling me just before bedtime that Freddy Krueger would come in my dreams with his long claws and kill me.

"Exactly. They had a thing for that. They kept singing. 'One, two, he is coming' ...And then he came."

"Who did?"

"Freddy."

"How is that?"

She shook her head and looked down. "One of them must have dressed up exactly like him. He was there in front of me. The same clothes, the red and black striped shirt, that brown hat and the glove, with the claws on the fingers. The person even wore a Freddy Krueger mask, so he looked exactly like him. I started to scream, and they said we were out in the ocean, so no one would ever hear me. It was like they wanted to hear me scream. They encouraged me to do it. So I did. That was all I could do —cry and scream. They told me they would stab me with the claws, that they would rip my body open. And then they cut me with them."

She lifted up her shirt. Long stripes of scars all over her chest were a constant reminder to her of that night of horror. She could never escape it.

"And then they raped me. All night. One at a time. They just kept going until I was numb."

Irene was quiet for a long period of time. I just stared at her and didn't know what to say. I'd never heard a story like this before. For a moment, I thought about my daughter and wanted to lock her up until she was thirty. I tried to put myself in her parents' place, but it was too unbearable.

"I must have passed out at some point," Irene continued, "because when I woke up, I was lying in an old fishing boat at the port. I was bleeding everywhere. Some fishermen found me and called for an ambulance. I was in the hospital for four months."

I sighed and looked at her. She didn't indulge in self pity.

"I understand that you were pregnant?" I asked.

"Yes. The doctors discovered I was pregnant and removed it while I was still at the hospital. I haven't been able to have children since."

I nodded and thought again about my daughter. How fragile life was and how easy someone could just rip it apart.

"Then what did you do?"

"The police came to the hospital and took a report. I told them who had done it and what happened. They immediately arrested the six boys, including Didrik Rosenfeldt. But only a few hours later, they were all freed. My parents told me they had dropped the charges against them. They had gotten a visit from a couple of the parents and received a big check for three million dollars. I was told never to talk about it again. My dad closed the store and we all moved away from Karrebaeksminde."

"That must have been difficult for you. That your parents dropped the charges without asking you?"

All of a sudden, I thought about my sister. Had they paid off my parents too? Was that why they refused to report the rape attempt to the police? I didn't like the thought.

Irene shook her head. "It was tough, yes, but I understood why. We would never stand a chance against those rich families in court. They would have the biggest, most expensive lawyers money could buy, and they would have won. Money can get you out of anything. They would find a way, and we would be left with nothing but the shame. At least we got enough money that my parents never had to work again."

I nodded, but felt everything inside me scream. What about the fact of trying to stop these guys from doing the same thing to someone else? Didn't that count for anything? Was money really that important? But, of course, I kept it to myself. I knew that to a lot of people in this world money meant everything.

Irene looked at me after wiping away a tear in her eye. "That's it. That's the story," she said.

I nodded again.

"I never saw them again, and hopefully never will."

I smiled and thought that, while she had to live with the scars for the rest of her life, the boys from the boarding school continued their lives as if nothing had happened. That was the power of money. I was disgusted and, more than ever, I wanted to print the story in my paper. I wanted to disgrace Didrik Rosenfeldt's name, and I didn't care what his son would say.

Irene interrupted my thoughts. "By the way, I actually have a picture from that evening," she said, as she stood up and left the room. She returned after a little while with an old photograph in her hand. She handed it to me.

"Didrik took it just before we got on the boat. The camera had a timer on it, so we could all get in the picture."

I took the picture. It showed six boys in white and blue Lacoste polo shirts. They were all smiling with their arms around each other. And in the middle of them stood Irene in her white summer dress, smiling with her bright white teeth. Off to have the time of her life. At least that's what she thought at the time.

"How did you get this?"

"Didrik sent it to me while I was still in the hospital."

What nerve that prick had.

"Can you please tell me their names, and can I borrow this?" I asked.

"Keep it."

11

We got back to the newspaper about lunchtime, and I sent Sune to a nearby café to get some sandwiches. I had opened my computer and started typing, when I sensed something was going on with Sara. She was so quiet, sitting there with her headphones on, just staring with an empty look in her eyes. I stood up and walked to her desk. She lifted a finger and put it over her lips to ask me to be quiet. She was definitely onto something. I waited a few seconds until she took off the headphones. She looked at me with excitement in her brown eyes.

"There has been one more," she said.

"Another murder?"

"Yes. The police are freaking out. They have never seen anything like this before, they keep saying."

I sat down on the corner of her desk. "I'll be damned..."

"You can say that again. Looks like we've got ourselves a real serial killer."

I nodded speculatively. "Any names yet?"

"Victim's name is Henrik Holch. Son-in-law of the creators and owners of DECCO shoes. He was the CEO of the company."

I got up in a hurry and rushed over to my desk. In my bag, I found the picture Irene had given me. I looked at the back where she had written the names of the six who raped her that night on the boat.

Henrik Holch was the last guy on the right. A slim blond boy with lots of pimples and a bright smile. And a bright future to go with it, I thought. I felt dizzy. I had actually found a connection between the two murders. So I picked up the phone and called Michael Oestergaard. He was busy, he said. But he would love to talk to me another time, just not right now.

"I have a connection between the two murders," I said.

He got quiet on the other end. "How do you even know there's been another murder? We haven't told the press yet. I just got here myself."

"Doesn't matter. The two murders are linked. They used to go to the same school. Herlufsholm boarding school. And they used to hang out together all summer. Down on Didrik Rosenfeldt's parents' boat. They were both accused of raping a girl in 1985 on that boat."

Michael was very quiet on the other end, and then he spoke with a little harshness in his voice. "Let us do the investigating, okay? I don't know where you got all that from, but we don't think the murders are related. They are too different in modus operandi, in the way the victims are killed. There doesn't seem to be any link between them according to our investigation. You are a reporter, so write that in your paper. Goodbye." He hung up.

I put the phone back in the cradle, stunned at his sudden change of attitude. Why didn't he want to see a connection between the murders?

Sune entered the editorial room with the sandwiches. I explained everything to him while we ate.

"Maybe he's afraid you'll write there's a serial killer on the loose, and that would create a lot of panic in the little town of Karrebaeksminde." Sune spoke with his mouth full and made me smile.

"You might be right. It would cause a lot of disturbance and anxiety among the locals."

"And keep the tourists away."

I nodded. He was right. Spring was on its way, and with it came a lot of tourists, and all the rich people from up north came to live in their summer residences. People came in their boats and ate fish on rye bread at the port, drinking beer and schnapps. That was a big deal for the small town. A lot of businesses survived only because of them. It would be a disaster if they stayed away.

But inside of me, thoughts buzzed around. Who was killing the boys from the picture? Could it be Irene Hansen finally getting her revenge?

I WROTE my article about Didrik Rosenfeldt, along with another one about the other murder of a high-profile businessman and a small story about who he was. I didn't mention the connection between the two killings I had discovered, since I didn't want to scare people, and I certainly didn't want to make detective Michael Oestergaard mad at me. I needed a good contact at the police. That was worth a lot.

Sara had left me a note on my desk that Giovanni Marco had called three times while I was with Irene Hansen. I decided not to call him back. He probably just wanted to know when the article about him would be in the paper, and frankly, with all that was going on, I didn't know when there would be room for it in the paper. I just told Sara if he called again to tell him we needed a picture of him and to make an appointment with Sune to go take it.

After that, I went home early and spent the rest of the day with my beautiful daughter and my beloved old father. That was a very popular decision at home. We really enjoyed each other's company, playing games, talking, eating, and laughing. Julie said she had a great day at school, and that melted my worried heart. She had made a new friend in her class. His name was Tobias. While she told me every-thing about her new friend, I thanked God for my daughter. No matter how angry I was with her dad, he had given me her, and for that I was eternally grateful to him.

12

Julie had nightmares that night and she climbed into my bed. I hugged her and lay close to her until she fell asleep again, but didn't get much sleep myself after that. My mind wandered.

I lay still in the bed, looking at the ceiling, just as I used to do as a kid. It hadn't changed. I knew every crack, every line in that ceiling, and they were all still there. I smiled to myself, feeling happy about some things staying the same. And then I thought about the murder cases. I was excited about having found the connection. But how did I move on from here? Should I just let it go and let the police do the work, like detective Michael Oestergaard wanted me to? But how could I? I felt strangely attached to the case, and I knew something important. What if I could stop the killer from striking again? What if I could follow the investigation so closely I would be the only journalist to break the story about the first serial killer in Denmark? The thought excited me.

And I knew exactly how I was going to do it.

AFTER DROPPING Julie off at her school the next morning, I drove to the nearest furniture store before I drove to the newspaper. I bought a desk and a chair and brought it all with me in the car. Then I bought a laptop in another store and called Sune and asked him to meet me in front of the newspaper. When I arrived, he stood outside and was waving at me. I asked him to help me get it all up the stairs.

Inside in the editorial room, we put the desk and chair down and unpacked it. It needed to be put together, so Sune helped me, while Sara looked at us in disbelief.

Finally, when it was done, we placed the desk next to mine and I smiled at Sune.

"Congratulations, this is your new workspace," I said to him.

He looked at me.

"What?"

"I want you to work with me on this case."

"How?"

"I need you to monitor the police work. Check the files, read the autopsy reports, and so on."

His eyes were now big and wide. "Are you kidding me?"

"Nope."

"You want me to hack into the police's main server and look at their files. Are you insane?"

"I might be."

Sune sighed loudly.

"I would love to—you know I really love that stuff—but I can't...I mean, if the police caught me...Once is one thing, but several times makes the possibility of being caught so much bigger."

"How would they ever know? You said yourself that you were good at it, that you could do it without leaving a trace. I bought you a brand new laptop. It belongs to the paper, so we will all get in trouble if anyone finds out."

Sune scratched his head. "I don't know..."

I suddenly felt bad, pushing him into doing something illegal. I didn't want him to get in trouble because of me, that was for sure.

"You know what? It was a bad idea." I closed the laptop. I sat down at my own desk. "Just forget it."

I opened my own laptop and checked my e-mails. Sune stood for a long time and stared at the empty desk. Then he sat down.

"Okay, but only on this case," he said. "Never again."

I smiled and handed him the laptop. "That's a promise."

It didn't take Sune long to find the autopsy reports of the two murders. He opened the files and showed them to me, starting with Didrik Rosenfeldt's. It made me sick to my stomach. I was about to vomit when I saw the pictures of Didrik Rosenfeldt's body. The housekeeper had been right in her description. It did look like a wild beast had ripped his body apart. It didn't look like something a human being would be capable of doing. The body was almost unrecognizable. Only the red hair revealed it was Didrik Rosenfeldt.

I studied the pictures for awhile and Sune helped me, even though I could tell his stomach had a hard time too. It took us a little longer than it probably should have, but finally we looked at each other.

"Look at the cuts," I said and pointed at Didrik Rosenfeldt's chest.

"It looks exactly like..." Sune said, but stopped.

"I know. Like the ones on Irene Hansen's chest. Except these seem deeper."

"Exactly."

"What does that mean?"

Sune shook his head. "I don't know. Could it be the same guy, maybe? The same one who dressed up like Freddy Krueger and mutilated her body?"

"That sounds possible. But why? As far as her story goes, they were all very good friends on that boat."

"I know."

"Let's look at Henrik Holch's file." I noted on a piece of paper the cause of Didrik Rosenfeldt's death was described in his file as death by stabbing.

With a few clicks, Sune found the other file.

"This one is not much better," he said before opening it.

I nodded. I figured that.

The pictures on the screen were awful. But it didn't look like Didrik Rosenfeldt's or the cuts on Irene Hansen. That disappointed me. Maybe the police were right after all. Maybe there was no other connection between the two killings than the fact that they went to the same school. Could that really be a coincidence? I didn't believe it one bit. The killer had just changed his pattern. His modus operandi, as the police called it. Maybe he had a reason for doing it. I asked Sune to let me read the rest of the file and he found it for me.

Apparently, the killer had cut off Henrik Holch's private parts, castrated him, so to speak. And then he had left him tied up to a chair, bleeding to death.

I leaned back in the chair. What a way to leave this world. But why did the killer choose that exact way of killing Henrik Holch? Why not just rip up his body like he did with Didrik Rosenfeldt? Did he have a reason? I scrolled in the file and found my answer.

"Bingo," I said.

"What?" Sune looked at me.

"He was a pedophile."

"How do you know?"

I pointed at a line on the screen.

"He was killed while watching child porn on his flat-screen TV."

Sune looked impressed.

"So you think the killer chose a different way of killing Henrik Holch because he was into having sex with children?"

"Yes."

"Like a punishment?"

"Something like that."

"So the first one was a bastard treating people poorly, having several affairs and just being a real prick all of his life, while the second one was a disgusting pedophile. Both of them were involved in the rape of Irene Hansen."

"Exactly."

"So someone is actually doing the world a favor?"

"You could put it like that, yes."

I paused before continuing. "The question is, which asshole will be next?"

13

In my mind, Irene Hansen could definitely be a suspect. She had the best motive for killing these guys, eliminating them one by one as revenge. But, somehow, I couldn't really see that skinny quiet woman being able to take down these men all by herself. Maybe she wasn't alone? She had a husband. Maybe he could have helped her. It was certainly a possibility.

My plan now was to find the rest of the men in the picture. To my surprise, headquarters loved my story about Didrik Rosenfeldt and wanted to run it in the morning paper. I expected to hear from Junior immediately after that. I cleared it with my editor and told him about the unpleasant visit the other day, but he said that I shouldn't worry about that. The Rosenfeldts did own the company that owned the newspaper, but they weren't supposed to be meddling in the editorial decisions. They had to go through him first, he said.

So I promised him another story about the six boarding school boys who raped Irene Hansen, a follow-up story to the first article. A "where are they now?" kind of article. I liked the idea. They raped a local girl, got away with it, and now they were living the sweet life of rich men.

"Make a small profile of each of them. The public will be interested in knowing who we have running around in our country, who they really are, especially since they all are very influential," my editor said.

So I was free to go after the boarding school boys.

I couldn't ask them about the rape. I had promised Irene not to blow her cover. She was hiding from them and told her story anonymously. But I could ask them about the two guys who were already dead.

IT DIDN'T TAKE Sune long to find the first one, Ulrik Gyldenlove. He lived in Klampenborg in northern Zeeland, north of Copenhagen, the richest part of the country. I called him and told him I was doing a story about two of his old friends from school. I wanted to talk to him about them, and much to my surprise, he agreed to meet with me.

We were to meet at Mattssons Riding Club next to Dyrehaven. It took about an hour and a half to get there. Dyrehaven was a famous area in Klampenborg. It was a big forest and had the richest animal wildlife in Denmark. It was famous for its many kinds of deer, and especially for a big hunt that takes place every first Sunday in November. Hubertusjagten, as it was called, was an old traditional hunt that was more than a hundred years old. It was inspired by the old traditional English hunts, with the riders wearing red jackets and using fox hounds. Nowadays they didn't use the hounds anymore or chase a real fox. Instead, they had equipped two riders with a fox tail on the shoulder and then the rest of the riders were supposed to catch the tail.

The event was always broadcast on TV and people would flock to the park to see the hunt every year. Some of the riders always ended up in an especially muddy pond. People would gather around the pond in order to see who it would be this year, who would end their hunt in a pile of mud, ruining their nice red jacket.

Ulrik Gyldenlove had just finished riding his horse for the day together with his daughter and they both got off when I approached and told them who I was. I told Sune to take some pictures of him with his beautiful horse and we chatted briefly with his twenty-year-old daughter before we went for a walk in the forest.

There was fog everywhere and it felt cold and damp on my skin. Between the trees, I now and then spotted movement. I couldn't tell if it was a deer or another animal, but there was definitely something in there.

Ulrik Gyldenlove had only lost a bit of his hair since the picture was taken at the port. He had gotten older and wasn't as slim as back then. But I recognized the look in his eyes, and his smile when he now and then showed me one. He seemed burdened, as though life had been hard on him. That surprised me. I had expected him to be more like Didrik Rosenfeldt, caring more for himself than others. But this guy was different.

As we walked slowly along a path in the forest, looking at the wildlife, he sighed deeply.

"This is my favorite spot in the whole world," he said and took in a deep breath of the moist air. "So quiet and calm."

I nodded. It was truly beautiful.

He looked at me with a smile.

"So how did you know I used to be friends with Didrik and Henrik? I haven't seen any of them in ages. We can hardly call each other friends anymore."

"Why haven't you seen each other for so long?" I asked, deliberately avoiding answering his question.

"Oh, I don't know. It's been so many years. Time flies. We went to the same school for years and I have tried to watch everybody's careers from a distance, but we haven't seen each other since the day we graduated."

"Why do you think that is?"

He shook his head. "We were just school buddies. We really didn't have that much in common."

We walked down the path for awhile in silence. Then I took out Irene's picture from the pocket in my brown leather jacket. I showed it to him.

He stopped and stared at it for a long time.

"How did you get that picture?" he said.

"It doesn't matter. What does matter is that you seem to be much more than just school buddies in this picture."

He sighed deeply and put a hand to his forehead. He seemed a bit preoccupied for a second.

"What is it you want from me?" he asked.

"I want to know about your friends. What were they like? My sister used to date Didrik Rosenfeldt for a short while, and she told me you and your friends acted out a lot when you came to Karrebaeksminde on summer vacation in the Rosenfeldt's residence. That you harassed people in the port area, and I know that you were at one point accused of having raped a girl on the boat."

Ulrik Gyldenlove sighed again.

"I just want to know the truth," I continued.

"You must do your research a little better next time," he said, handing me the picture back. "The charges were all dropped. There was no case against us. They were false accusations. The poor girl must have been mentally ill or something."

"It was dropped because you paid her family off. Don't think I didn't do my research," I said, suddenly afraid of having said too much. Would they go after Irene for this?

He sighed again. "It's such a long time ago. Why dig up the past now? Why can't you just leave it alone?"

"Because someone is killing your old school buddies and it might be because of something you did back then. For all I know, you might be next."

He looked at me with serious eyes. "Don't you think I have been asking myself that?"

14

Ulrik Gyldenlove was quiet for a long period of time while we walked on the path. I had borrowed a pair of Wellies at the Riding Club and they made a funny squelching sound when I walked. We reached Erimitageslottet, a small castle that never was used for royalty to live in, but as a place for the king to have his banquet for the riders of the hunt. It was placed on the highest point of the forest, overlooking all of the beautiful landscape.

It had a lot of history. I sensed that as we passed it.

"Most of the other students were afraid of that group," he said suddenly without looking at me. He stared out at the wide landscape that opened up between the trees. A herd of deer were gathered not far from us. One looked up and stared back at us.

"They enjoyed it. They liked to make people scared of them," he continued. "The school was their domain. And a lot of the other students got a taste of their tough love. They had a reputation of being like wild animals."

"What do you mean by they 'got a taste of their tough love'?"

"They beat them up. Sometimes half to death."

"Why?"

He looked at me. "For fun." He looked away again. "They got some kind of pleasure out of it. Sometimes there was no reason at all for them to pick on some poor kid and beat the crap out of him. He was just at the wrong place at the wrong time."

"I don't think I understand."

"What is there to understand? They were just pure evil. They wanted to be evil."

"But weren't they afraid of being kicked out of school? Didn't their parents send them there to get a good education and a bright future?"

"You don't know a lot about boarding schools, do you?"

"I'm sure I don't."

"Boarding schools are used for rich parents to get rid of their kids. Sending them to boarding school means they don't have to deal with them any longer. Most rich parents are emotionally inadequate, almost disabled. Because their own parents didn't love them, they are not capable of loving their children. So, they ship them off to boarding school and only have to spend time with them on the holidays. And even then, they are too busy for them. So they are left to themselves. Rich and merciless. Without any compassion for other human beings, since they haven't gotten any growing up. That's the life of most boarding school kids. They did indeed want to amount to something. But they knew they would on account of their parents. And everybody knew if you wanted to be someone when school was over, you'd better not have pissed these guys off while you were in school. If you were friends with Didrik Rosenfeldt, you would surely amount to something later in life."

"But you're not like that. You're different, why?"

"I broke off with them in 1986. Told them I didn't want to be a part of their game anymore. It was over for me."

"Game?"

He sighed again. I sensed that he had been running from this story most of his adult life, thinking he could escape it, but now it had caught up to him.

"They had a game called 'A Gentleman Hunt'."

"A Gentleman Hunt? What was that?"

"It was a game that Didrik Rosenfeldt invented. One of the guys would come up with a fantasy and they would go out and make it real. Like raping the girl while dressed as Freddy Krueger. It was a challenge. Someone would challenge the rest of the group to do something awful, and then they had to do it. If one refused, they would be beaten up and thrown out of the game. To be excluded from the group meant no protection. You were certain to be their next victim."

"How did he come up with that?"

"One time he told us he had this fantasy about scaring the shit out of a boy in eighth grade, and then he told the rest of the group what he wanted to do to him, and then they all went out and did it."

"What did they do?"

"The kid was from the U.S. He had lost his parents in a car accident and had this one picture of them he always kept close to him, in his pocket. Didrik and the rest took the picture from him one afternoon in the boys' bathroom. They took it from his clothes while the kid was in the shower. When he came out, naked, they showed him they had taken it. He wanted it back and started crying, but they didn't care. They stuck the picture in his mouth and lit it on fire. He was to hold it like that. If he dropped it, they would shoot him, they said, and they placed a gun to the boy's head. As the picture burned, the crying boy eventually burned himself and dropped the burning picture to the floor."

"Then what?"

"Then they pulled the trigger. But it clicked. It wasn't loaded."

"Wow. That was tough."

"The boy had to leave the school after that."

"What about Didrik Rosenfeldt and his gang?"

"Their parents paid the victim off and they continued their lives. And that was just the beginning. Then they started picking on all the new students who came to the school. Challenging each other in various fantasies and making them real."

"Someone must have complained about them to the headmaster."

"Some did every once in a while. And they paid the price for it. I remember one in particular who told on the boys, and they hung him from the ceiling in the gym, by his arms. Then they beat him all night like a punching bag. He had to spend six months in the hospital. And he never told anyone who did it."

Ulrik looked up and spotted a falcon looking for food on the ground. He pointed at it and I saw it too. The fog had gotten lighter and we could now see more of the forest.

"Did they pick on you?" I asked.

"You only pick on someone who won't fight back."

I nodded.

"But I could have stopped them," he then said. "I should have."

WE BEGAN to walk back to the riding club. I had promised Sune I wouldn't take too long, since we had a long drive home, and he had to pick up his son.

"You have a son?" I asked in surprise.

"Yes, I do."

"You didn't tell me that."

"Well, you didn't ask."

His son was apparently seven years old. Sune was only nineteen when they had him. The boy's mother had been young too, and she didn't want the child. So he was a single dad.

I was stunned at the way people kept surprising me lately and wondered what else he had kept from me as we walked back in silence. I also wondered about this group of boarding school kids who had terrorized the whole school for years without any consequences. I wondered what role Ulrik Gyldenlove had in it and how I was supposed to put it all in an article without putting Irene Hansen's life at risk. I would have to discuss it with Ole, my editor, when we got back. We reached the riding club, where Sune was waiting for us with Ulrik's daughter.

"Can I see the picture again?" Ulrik asked, just as we were about to leave.

I got it out of my pocket and handed it to him.

He stared at it and I saw sadness in his eyes.

"These two are dead now," he said and pointed at Didrik Rosen-feldt and Henrik Holch.

I nodded.

"Then there are only three of us left."

I looked surprised at him.

"You mean four, right?"

He put his finger on another boy's face in the photo.

"No. This guy, Bjorn Clausen, killed himself in 1987. That means there are only three left."

15

So one of the boarding school boys was already dead. But how did he die? I searched the internet when we got back to Karrebaeksminde, and all the newspapers at the library. And I had Sune find anything he could on Bjorn Clausen and his suicide in 1987 from the internet and the police archives. But all we got was a small note in the local paper and an old report from the police of what was a closed case, definitely suicide.

Jumped off of a bridge in front of a train.

I had run dry of ideas. Who was that guy? I asked myself and looked at the picture. Brown hair, blue eyes. Tall, muscular. He looked a bit familiar to me, but I couldn't quite place him.

I decided to let it go and concentrated on my article, while Sune went to get his son. I told him he could drop his son off at my dad's and he would take care of him while we were working.

Sune called me after he had dropped off his son. I learned his son was Tobias, Julie's new best friend in school, so that turned out to be a very popular decision. I was getting quite good at this small-town life. I asked Sune to bring pizza when he came back.

Jumping off of a bridge and getting hit by a train was certainly an effective way of killing yourself. But why? He was nineteen. He had just graduated from high school six months before. Was it just teenage depression? Ulrik Gyldenlove had described him as a cold-hearted player of a game where they would beat the living hell out of kids that were younger than them and rape a local girl just for the fun of it. Had he had some regrets? Some kind of conscience? Was he unable to keep on living, knowing what he and his friends had done? It sounded a bit unlikely to me.

"Maybe the killer had already begun looking to get revenge back in 1987," Sune said with cheese from the pizza on his lip.

I signaled with my finger on my own lip, and he removed it.

"That's possible. But why wait twenty-four years before killing the next?"

"I don't know," Sune said with his mouth full.

"Maybe the killer has been away. Maybe he was sent to college somewhere out of the country. Maybe in England or in the U.S.?"

Sune nodded. "That sounds likely. A lot of these kids went on to become big-shots later in life, and often they would have to go to foreign countries in order to get the best education money could buy before they came back and took over the family business."

"Exactly," I said.

"But that doesn't help us much," he said with a grin.

"What do you mean?"

"After what you told me today, almost every kid in that school could have a potential motive for killing them. A lot of kids were beaten and harassed and would like to get their revenge at some point."

"You're right," I said heavily. "There could be hundreds of potential killers out there wanting to get rid of Didrik Rosenfeldt and his gang."

Sune took another piece of pizza from the box.

"So what do we do now?" He leaned back in his chair while eating.

"What is there to do?"

"Don't ask me."

"First, I'll write my article on the boarding school boys and where they are now. And then I will write another article on the harassment. I made a deal with Gyldenlove that I wouldn't use his name, thereby telling the rest of the gang that he is the one who ratted them out. I'll just call him an anonymous source from the school. Then I am going to e-mail the articles to my editor in Naestved. He is waiting for them and promised to read them right away and then put them in the paper."

"And then?"

"Then I will be going home to my family. My daughter is supposed to be sound asleep by then, but since Tobias is there with her, she will most likely be fully awake, running around having the time of her life. I will then tuck her in, after saying goodbye to you and Tobias."

"Then what do we do with the case?"

"What is there left to do but to wait for the killer to strike again?"

AN HOUR or so later the door suddenly buzzed to the editorial room. Sune got up and let someone in. It was Giovanni Marco. He had come to get his picture taken for the article. He had made the appointment with Sune, since he was already in town doing some other business.

I smiled at him, and said hi, but didn't pay any more attention to him. I was busy with my articles. Sune asked him to stand against a wall and then he took a lot of different pictures of him.

Then they went outside to get some photos of him with some of his work displayed in town. Before they left, Giovanni approached me.

I looked up and into his blue eyes. He smiled his handsome smile.

"I am sorry you threw away my phone number," he said with that cute irresistible Italian accent.

"Who said I threw it away?"

"I just figured, since you didn't call me back."

"Well, I didn't."

"Okay, then," he said and turned away.

"Okay."

He stopped himself and looked at me again. "Then maybe you would consider having dinner with me some day?"

I blushed and hoped he didn't notice.

"I might consider that."

"I will call you, then."

IT WAS LATE when Sune and I got to my dad's home. Sune had been researching Bjorn Clausen for hours, while I wrote the stories for the newspaper. The editor had read them and loved them right away. They would be in the morning paper, he said.

When we got inside we both had quite a scare. Inside in the living room stood two men twice the size of Sune. My dad was sitting on the couch, looking at us with fear in his eyes.

"Dad, are you okay?" I yelled and ran across the room. I kneeled in front of him and looked him in the eyes.

He nodded and took my hand.

"I'm fine, sweetheart. I'm fine."

"Where are the kids?"

"They're upstairs. They're sleeping. Don't worry about them."

I breathed a sigh of relief and got back to my feet. I looked at the two guys staring at me and started yelling at them. "Who are you? And what the hell are you doing here?"

One of the men looked at me. "Peter sent us."

I froze. Sune looked at me. He grabbed my arm.

"Are you okay? Who is Peter?"

I looked at the tall bald guy with broad shoulders. I knew his type. He didn't scare me.

"Well, then you can tell Peter to just butt out of my life. Out of our lives. I don't want anything to do with him ever again."

"Peter wants to see his daughter."

"Tell him I don't care. I don't want her to be among criminals. I want her to have the ordinary life of an ordinary girl."

I stepped a couple of steps in the big guy's direction while I kept yelling at him. The worst I could do right now was to show fear. Peter could never know that I was afraid of him. He would use it against me...manipulate me into coming back.

I opened the door and showed the men out.

"You go tell him that."

16

"You have some explaining to do, young lady."

My dad stood by the stove in the kitchen the next morning when I came down. Julie had been sleeping when I woke up, so I let her sleep a little longer. After all, it was Saturday and she didn't have school.

I sat down at the table. I felt like I was thirteen years old again and my parents had caught me smoking.

"Can't it wait?" I said, looking at my watch. I had promised Sune to go to the newspaper and look at the pictures he had taken of Giovanni Marco and choose three of them for the article about him.

My dad looked at me with discontent.

"I need to know. What happened to you two? You and Peter were so happy?"

I sighed. My dad poured me a cup of coffee and put it in front of me.

"It's really a long story, Dad..."

He sat down with his own cup. "I have nothing but time."

I sighed again and took his hand. I smiled. How I loved my talks with him when I was younger. I used to be able to tell him everything.

He was nothing like my mom and sister, who were always so judgmental.

"You know we met in Iraq, right?"

My dad nodded.

"He was a soldier?"

"Actually, he was an officer. I went there as a reporter and lived on the base. That's how we met. He took care of me, helped me get my stories for the paper, knew who I should talk to, and got me different interviews with the local people. I wasn't allowed to go anywhere on my own. That was way too dangerous, with all the kidnapping of foreign journalists going on at that time. So his soldiers arranged to escort me everywhere I needed to go."

"And then you fell in love?"

"Yes. We grew fond of each other. He actually saved my life at one point."

My dad looked seriously at me. "You never told me that!"

"I didn't want to worry you."

"Well, it's a little too late for that."

"I know. I never meant for you to be concerned."

"Then you shouldn't have gone to Iraq in the first place," he said with smile.

I smiled back and drank my coffee.

"Anyway, through my Iraqi interpreter, I got promised an interview with one of the leaders of Al-Qaeda, a general high up in the hierarchy. It was a really big scoop for me. I had already become a big name from my previous articles about the war, but this one would put me over the top. My career would have been secured after that. But Peter wouldn't let me go. He said it was too dangerous because I had to go there alone without any protection."

"Well, of course it was too dangerous. Are you kidding me? Did you really consider going?"

"I didn't just consider. I went. Without Peter's approval."

"You always were a stubborn little girl." Dad laughed, yet with obvious seriousness in his eyes.

"I know. No one could tell me what to do, right?"

"Right."

"Anyway, I went, and of course it was a setup. There was no general there. Instead, I got a black hood over my head and was thrown into the back seat of a car. I kicked and screamed, but in a town like Bagdad, no one would hear, and if they did, no one would react."

"More coffee?" Dad stood up and poured us both a second cup. I could tell it was hard for him to hear this story.

"I felt the car moving and tried to listen to the sounds around me, trying to locate where we were going. I knew they would probably take me to the mountains and hide me in a house far away until my ransom was paid. That's what they usually did. But I also knew the chances of anyone paying the ransom were very small, since all nations participating in the war had agreed not to cave in to the pressure of terrorists. And then the kidnappers would probably have to kill me."

"Wow, I am glad I didn't hear about this until now," Dad said.

"Me too."

"So, what happened? How did you get away?"

"The car hadn't gotten far from the town when it crashed. I couldn't see what it was, but it felt big. I heard my kidnappers yelling a lot, but I didn't understand a word, except the Arabic word for soldiers they kept yelling to each other. I sensed that hope wasn't all lost. I started yelling that I was in the car on the passenger seat and I heard the door open and someone dragged me out and took the black hood off of me. It was Peter. They had followed me anyway to the meeting with the alleged general and saw me being dragged out in the car. Then they crashed a van into the car carrying me and scared off the kidnappers."

My dad leaned back in the chair. "I always knew I liked the guy."

I smiled. Dad got up, got the toast, and put it in front of me. I buttered it and put cheese on it. The way I always liked it.

Dad looked like he enjoyed watching me eat. He had a fried egg and poured a lot of salt on it.

"Easy on the salt there," I said. "I need you to stay alive for a little while."

"You're beginning to sound like your mother."

"That might be, but you had a stroke, remember? At the top of the stairs. The stroke didn't finish you off, but you could easily have killed yourself falling down instead."

"That doesn't mean I can't eat salt. That just means I should stay away from stairs," he said with a big smile and took a bite of the egg.

I laughed and ate.

"But you still haven't explained why things went wrong with you two," he said after a little while.

"Well, I got pregnant while we were still at the base, and that complicated things. I told the paper and they sent me home. Peter came back after two months and we got married."

"That, I remember. I am glad your mother got to see you in that white dress before she died. You looked so happy."

"I was."

"So, what the hell happened to you?"

"I had the baby and everything was perfect until Peter had to go again."

"To Iraq?"

"Yes, he was deployed for another six months. When he got back, something horrible had happened to him. I didn't recognize him any longer. He screamed and cried at night. He got raging mad over small things, and he couldn't take being home in boring little Denmark. It was like he didn't know how to live a normal life any longer."

"PTSD?"

"Something like that. I'm not sure, but he wasn't himself anymore. I couldn't rely on him. And he wouldn't talk to me about it. He cried when he thought I wasn't listening, he would get so mad he would throw things around, and he even hit me a few times. Not hard, just slapped me a couple of times."

"He did not!"

"It's okay; I wasn't hurt, but I started speculating about Julie. Was this the kind of upbringing that I wanted for her?"

"So you came down here?"

"Not yet. First he went away again to Iraq. I pleaded and begged with him to stay home, but he said he had to go, that it was his duty. And I just gave up on him. I thought I at least would have six months of peace and a quiet normal life for me and Julie. And we did have almost a normal life for a couple of months, until I found something. I hadn't heard from him in a long time, so I wondered what he was up to. I opened his e-mail account and read all of his latest e-mails. I thought I would see letters from a woman or discover he was having an affair or something."

"But that wasn't what you found?"

"What I found made me so scared and so mad at him. It appeared that he wasn't in Iraq as a soldier in the Danish army. He had started his own private security company in Iraq with several of the soldiers from his battalion who had left the army with him."

"So, what was the problem?"

"Peter had told me before about these so-called security companies. The name is just a cover up. They don't secure anything or keep anyone safe. They are mercenaries. They kill people for money."

My dad stopped eating and looked at me. "That can't be true. Peter wouldn't...?"

"Apparently, he would."

"So, what did you do?"

"I confronted him when he got back. And he didn't take it well. He locked me and Julie in the basement for a week. That was his answer. He didn't even defend himself."

"Oh, my God, sweetheart," he said and held my hand.

"It's okay, Dad, don't worry. We're fine now, remember?"

"How did you get out?"

"Eventually, he opened the door and let us out. We had to promise never to bring it up again or he would have to lock us back in the basement. I was really afraid of him after that and realized I couldn't live like that. He was a ticking bomb. So one day when I was supposed to be at work, I packed all I could, and Julie and I came down here. The rest of the story you know."

My dad had a tear in the corner of his eye. I got up and gave him a hug.

"I'm so sorry I wasn't there for you. I thought you were just having the usual problems couples go through when they have kids. I'm so glad you came to me."

"Me too," I said, still hugging him.

"What are you doing?" Julie had sneaked up on us in the kitchen.

I wiped a tear from my eye and let go of my dad.

"Nothing sweetheart. Grandpa is just so glad we are here," I said.

"So you started crying?"

"Well, yes. I missed him too, you know. Sometimes people get emotional."

She made an annoyed face and sat down at the table.

"Grownups are weird."

17

L illy, the cat, sat on my bed while I was trying on dresses. I had
spent a few hours at the newspaper with Sune, when Giovanni
Marco called my cell phone and asked if I would have dinner with him
at his house at the beach on Enoe. In my head, I had a ton of excuses,
but finally I ended up accepting his invitation.

I suddenly envied the simplicity of the cat's life. Eating, sleeping,
eating, licking herself clean. She just liked to relax and take it easy,
with no complications in her life. Unlike me. This dinner could end
up complicating my life even more than it already was, and I didn't
exactly need that right now.

I finally headed downstairs wearing a purple dress that was a little
tight, but really showed off my figure. I was slim, but not skinny. Ever
since the pregnancy, I still had yet to lose around five pounds that kept
resisting my every effort to get rid of it. Not that it bothered me. I
wasn't one of those women who got their self-esteem from the way
they looked. And I had no idea how to go on a diet anyway. So I just
made peace with it. But every now and then, like now, I missed my old
body from before the pregnancy, when everything was in its proper
place. But by the look of my daughter and dad, I could tell that I wasn't
looking too bad.

"Wow, Mom! You look amazing. Very beautiful," my daughter said.

My dad smiled. "You'd better be careful with that man. He's not a real man if he doesn't try something with a stunning-looking woman like that."

"I'll be very careful; don't worry," I said, and kissed his cheek.

"Who is he? Tell me please who he is," Julie begged me.

I kissed her on the cheek too.

"Later, sweetheart. It's nothing but a dinner with a nice man I met through work. That's all it is."

"But why are you eating with him? What about Dad?"

The question I had dreaded. I was squatting in front of her, looking her directly in the eyes.

"It is just dinner. I promise you that."

"Okay."

I kissed her again and got up. "Do I look all right?"

"You are so beautiful, Mom."

"Thanks."

I knew I could trust her. Her eyes were like a mirror of truth. She would not hold back if she thought I looked horrible.

"Don't wait up," I said, and left the house as they waved at me.

I DROVE THERE, since I had no intention of drinking and losing control. As I pulled into the driveway of the beach house, I almost regretted my decision. I had just split up with my husband and I wasn't emotionally ready for anything new yet. And neither was Julie. She didn't need a new man in her life right now.

But then, I really liked the guy. Yes, he was a little too much into himself and his artistic work, but there was something incredibly sweet about him. And he had a way of being a real gentleman with me. He always held the door, a virtue a lot of Danish men had forgotten all about. He listened when I talked and he would actually remember what I said afterwards. I thought, maybe I just need to have someone spoil me for once, and went up to the door.

I got to be spoiled, all right. Barely had I set foot in his beach house before he placed me on the floor in a pile of huge pillows with a glass of red wine. Italian, of course, my favorite. Then he prepared dinner for us. Barefoot, of course. I drank some of the wine, saving the rest for dinner, since I could only have one glass if I was to drive home. And that was still my intention.

Dinner was amazing. He had set the table with candles and fresh flowers. And then he served the food.

"Tomatoes with balsámico vinegar di Módena, and buffalo mozzarella," he said in Italian and sat down in front of me. He wore a white shirt. The two top buttons were opened and I spotted a gold cross on a chain underneath. He was probably Catholic.

"Dig in."

I lifted my glass in a toast. "To le chef."

He smiled and we drank. As we started eating, he looked at me.

"What?"

"Nothing I just really like to watch you eat my food. You are not one of those women who won't eat."

"I am not, no," I said with my mouth full. "I love food. You won't be seeing me not being able to finish my salad and water."

He laughed.

"Well, I'm glad. Because the next dish is Rigatoni al Tartufo. And that is not for people who are afraid of a little butter and fat."

I smiled.

"What is it?"

"Rigatoni with tenderloin, truffles, and chanterelles."

My mouth was watering just at the very thought. "Bring it on."

OF COURSE, I couldn't just have one glass of that wonderful red wine, so when he offered me a second, I decided I would take a taxi home. Then I could enjoy the evening without having to think about drinking and driving. So I had one more glass, and a few more after that. After dinner, we sat on the pillows on the floor and he lit a fire in the fireplace. The beach and ocean were all black outside the big windows and it felt like looking right into nothingness.

"Do you want to feel the ocean breeze?" he asked.

"I would love to."

He put on a sweater and I got my big winter jacket, and then he opened the door to the porch and took my hand. The wind was freezing. It felt like it was biting my cheeks. I took in a breath of the fresh air.

"I just love this place," he said and looked out over the ocean.

I did too, I had to admit.

"Come, let's go all the way down to the ocean," he said all of a sudden, while pulling my hand.

Like a schoolgirl, I followed him. We ran to keep warm. When we got there, he stopped. The half moon rose over the water. Without a warning, Giovanni just grabbed me, pulled me near, and kissed me.

18

I woke up with the worst hangover in history. At least for me, that is. Not only did I have too much of that great Italian wine the night before, but I also woke up in Giovanni's bed. Something I had promised myself wouldn't happen. So the regrets were hurting more than the actual headache.

What had I done? What the hell was I thinking? Who is this guy anyway? I didn't know anything about him, and now I had slept with him. And what about Julie? She might have had a nightmare and tried to find me in my bed, but I wasn't there. Who would have comforted her?

I sat up in the bed. I was naked. My clothes were on the floor. Giovanni was still sleeping. It was only five thirty in the morning. I could hurry home and pretend like I had been home all night. It was not impossible.

I hurried and collected all my stuff and sneaked out. I felt like an idiot from some movie, but this was how I wanted to deal with this for now. I had to get away.

. . .

JULIE WAS STILL SLEEPING in her bed when I got back to the house half
an hour later. Quietly, I sneaked into my own bed and got under the
comforter. I even fell asleep for half an hour more before she woke
me up.

She stood beside my bed. Her arms were crossed in front of her
chest. I sat up.

"Morning, sweetheart. Did you sleep well?"

"Where have you been?"

Uh, oh.

"Come, sit," I said and patted the bed.

She sat down.

"I slept at that man's house. It was too late for me to drive all the
way home."

"But you promised that it would only be dinner."

"I know. But we were having a real nice time. He's really nice to
talk to. And then I forgot about the time."

"I sure wish you hadn't."

"I know."

"What about Dad, then? Who is going to eat with him now?"

I sighed. She was always so direct. "I don't know. I really don't
know, sweetie."

"Why are you still so mad at him? He said he was sorry for locking
us in the basement."

"But he also said he would do it again if we didn't do as he told us
to. I can't live like that. You'll understand when you get older. I'll
explain it then."

She reached out and took my hand. "I understand it now, Mommy.
I don't wanna go back in that basement either."

I smiled.

"Come here and kiss me, peaches," I said, and tried to grab her.

She laughed and screamed and ran out of the room. "Try to catch
me if you can."

· · ·

GIOVANNI CALLED a little later when we were in the middle of a big puzzle on the floor. All three of us were heavily concentrating on the project.

"You were gone when I woke up," he said with a gentle voice.

"I know; I'm sorry."

"No note or anything? That was brutal."

"I know. Sorry. I just needed to get back to my daughter."

"I understand. I just never had a woman sneak out on me before."

I laughed. "Well, there's a first time for everything."

"It's quite intriguing, I must say. It makes you mysterious and hard to get. I like that."

I laughed again. "I'm glad you do. 'Cause I really had a nice time last night."

"Me too. Let's do it again, then?"

"Let's do that."

19

Pastor Bertel Due-Lauritzen was a holy man. He knew God and had a personal relationship with him. Everything he did was directed by the Lord himself. At least, that is what he told himself when he hung up his collar at the end of the day. The kids in the juvenile detention center where he worked called him the Bishop, which he didn't mind too much, since he knew all are created equal in God's eyes. And, like a bishop, he worked for God. He was there to tell the juvenile criminals about God, that there was a way out for them and his name is Jesus. It wasn't too late for them to change.

In the very beginning, when he first came to the detention center, he had been very patient with the youngsters. Since it was a prison, he had made what he called a confessional chair in the prison church, even though he wasn't Catholic. But he found it useful for the kids to be able to talk to him anonymously about what they had done. What he didn't tell them was that he would always know who it was on the other side of the curtain he had put up.

When they came to confess their sins, he would nod and ask them to repent and ask for forgiveness, and then they would be off to do more damage. But they seemed to keep on getting themselves into trouble. Again and again, he had to ask for God's forgiveness in their lives, but nothing seemed to change. And he had a difficult time coping with the teasing behind his back. They would laugh at him when he gave them a Bible to read or when he would give them a Bible quote he thought might get them through the day.

"Remember, you are all children of God. He will forgive you and love you if you ask him to," he would say. But they wouldn't listen. No one would.

He had given up on his old lifestyle. He had to. He had given up his rich and wild life where everything was possible. Where the cars were big and the boats even bigger. After boarding school, he told his parents he didn't want to work for their company. He didn't want to end up like them. He told them he was gay and wanted them to accept it.

They had slammed the door right in his face. Called him a disgusting faggot and told him they never wanted to see him again. He was no longer their son.

After that, he had to get by without his parent's money for the first time in his life. He found love and helping hands in the gay bars of Copenhagen. Men brought him home and gave him money to have sex with them, and sometimes he even got to spend the night. He lived on the streets, selling his body to whoever wanted it, eating only whenever one of his clients was kind enough to buy him something at a bakery or a hotdog stand. And he thought he had deserved that life. He loathed himself. He hated that his sexuality had brought him into this mess. Why couldn't he just have oppressed it? Why did he have to blurt it all out in front of his parents?

One day, he had sex in an alley with a man who turned out to be a priest. He proved to be a really nice guy and they started talking afterwards. He told him he had known ever since he was a kid that he liked men. But he had learned not to express his sexuality in public.

"As a priest, no one would ever ask you why you don't have a wife and kids," he said. That gave Bertel an idea. Not only could he hide his ugly disgusting, impure thoughts from the world, maybe he would also be able to help someone else out of their miserable lives. Maybe even young kids who needed to be saved, as he had needed it, when God came along in form of a priest.

AFTER GETTING AN EDUCATION, with a little help from his friend from the alley, he got a job working at the juvenile detention center. But very soon, he realized he didn't make much difference in their lives. He reached out to them, but they didn't change. God didn't work in them and make them better. So he went to his altar and prayed about it.

"Why won't they change, God?" he asked. "Why do they keep laughing at me? Why won't they listen to your words?"

And he had gotten his answer. In God's own words. "So if your eye —even your good eye—causes you to lust, gouge it out and throw it away. It is better for you to lose one part of your body than for your whole body to be thrown into hell. And if your hand—even your stronger hand—causes you to sin, cut it off and throw it away."

Jesus had said it like that. So it had to be, then.

Pastor Bertel had then gone to one of the kids in the middle of the night and put acid in both of his eyes. Of course, he had sedated the kid first. He wasn't a monster. And then he had left him there for someone else to find. No one ever knew how it happened, but the kid never looked at a woman with lust again. And he never raped anyone again.

That's how he began his real work for God.

Sometimes, he would just teach the kids a lesson by beating them senseless and threatening them with death if they told anyone, and sometimes he had to go to more extreme methods in order to reach the youngsters. Sometimes he had to castrate someone to keep him from raping.

After a while, it had become even better than back at the boarding school when he and his friends used to beat other kids up, because this wasn't meaningless. This was to make someone's life better; this was working for God. And in the end, when it was all over, all that would matter was what he had done for him during his time on earth.

20

Pastor Bertel Due-Lauritzen had just ended his ten o'clock Sunday service. As usual, he would tell the juvenile criminals to come to the confession chair afterwards and tell him their sins. Now he was sitting in his chair, waiting for someone to show up on the other side of the curtain. He waited for a long time, but knew nothing would happen. Pastor Bertel sighed deeply. It was always the same.

In the calm of the prison church that day in February, he thought about the summers of years past. The smell of the sea, the laughter, sailing in the open water with his friends, the look on Bjorn's face just before he jumped with the other boys in the water naked. Sitting on the deck wanting to kiss Bjorn and touch his soft skin. The lost desires in the light summer night. The unfulfilled longings. The torture of being so close to someone you love and not being able to express your emotions. Because he knew they would have resented him for it. They would have hated him if they knew how he felt.

And Bjorn would have been the worst. He would have hated Bertel more than anything. Bjorn always was the strongest among them. He was the one with all the ideas. He came up with the Freddy Krueger rape. He even made that glove himself. He could do stuff like that.

Bjorn wasn't quite like the average boy in boarding school. He wasn't rich and he could make things with his hands. If they ever were deserted on a desert island, he would have been the only survivor. Not because he could have built a hut or caught food, but because he would have killed the others and eaten them. He was like that. He was a beast. The evilest among them. And Bertel had loved him. He had loved his strong, muscular arms and his beautiful strong face. He had even loved the beast inside of him.

And then Bjorn killed himself.

A few months after their graduation, he jumped off a bridge and was hit by a train. Bertel could never understand why he would do such a thing. It was incomprehensible. He had cried for days when he heard it. That was when he had decided to tell his parents the truth about himself. He couldn't hide it any longer. At least, that was what he thought.

Boy, had he been young and naïve.

BERTEL TOUCHED the rough fabric on the armchair and thought about the few times he had reached out and touched the skin on Bjorn's arm without him knowing why.

Suddenly, he felt the solitude was broken, that he was not alone in the church. A light step, almost noiseless was moving across the floor. Then calm, regular breathing behind the curtain. Pastor Bertel waited for the person behind the curtain to be ready. He looked under the curtain and saw the shoes, as he always did. He would memorize anything he could about them. Their color and shape and even the brand. Then he would later find them in the dining hall and know the face of the owner. But these shoes were different than the ones he normally saw under the heavy red curtain. Mostly, the youngsters wore sneakers or Converse. But these were shoes like the ones Bertel wore. Like a man of his own age would wear.

Bertel smelled the perfume of clean skin mixed with good cologne. And all of a sudden, he recognized the smell. That exact cologne that only his long lost love would wear. Bertel widened his eyes at the sound of the song long forgotten.

"Five, six, grab your crucifix..."

"Who are you?"

A moment of silence, and then the man answered in a deep resonant voice. "Does it matter?"

"Yes, it does."

"Who I am is of no importance."

"Then what is important?"

"Why I am here."

Pastor Bertel felt his throat constrict. The feeling of suffocation overwhelmed him. "I've read about you in the paper. You killed Didrik and Henrik. I figured you would come for me too. In a way, I've been waiting for you."

Bertel had an urge to get up and pull away the curtain to see his perpetrator's face. But something kept him from doing it. Some force bigger than himself forced him to stay in his chair. The same force that the boys in the juvenile prison had come to know after the nightly visits with the prison's pastor. The same force that would keep them awake night after night staring anxiously at the door to their cell. Afraid that it would open and they would once again lose a finger, an ear, be blinded, or even castrated.

It was fear.

"I suppose there's nothing I can do or say to make you change your mind?"

"You suppose right."

"So, it is over?"

A long motionless silence. For an instant, the pastor in the armchair thought the man behind the curtain was gone.

"Can I please at least see your face?"

Another silence from his perpetrator before the sound of the curtain being pulled aside filled the air. A face appeared on the other side. The glove from his past was pointing right at him. The pastor wasn't afraid any longer. But he was indeed surprised.

"So, it is you?"

"Yes."

"But why? Why now after all these years?"

"Because your time is up. The game is over."

The pastor was content with the answer. He had always known that the past that he had too long been running from, would one day catch up with him.

And this was it. His time was up. After all, he was a priest. He wasn't frightened by the end, only by the pain.

"Will I suffer?"

"Yes."

21

Sunday is supposed to be a day of rest. A day to spend with your loved ones. And so this Sunday began. But shortly after I hung up after talking to Giovanni, my phone rang again. This time it was Sara.

"There's been another one. Another murder, they say on the police radio."

She sounded so excited. They had never had a murder in this area before, and now they had three in one week.

"Aren't you supposed to have the day off?"

"I am. I'm at my house."

"So you have a police radio at your house too?"

"Well, of course. Most things happen on the weekends."

That was true, I had to admit.

"So tell me about the murder." I waved at my daughter, who wanted me to come back and do the rest of the puzzle with her. I signaled both her and my dad that this was important.

"You are never going to believe this. It's a priest this time."

"A priest?"

"In the juvenile prison."

"Where is that?"

"Roedvig Stevns."

"Now where is that exactly?"

"About an hour's drive from here. Just on the east coast of Zeeland."

In the middle of nowhere, that is, I thought.

"How do we know it is the same guy?"

"We don't. But the police keep talking about his chest being ripped apart. Using words like 'almost looks inhuman, beastlike, messy, blood everywhere.' I just thought you might like to check it out for yourself."

"You thought right," I said, and got the address of the juvenile prison. Now all I had to do was call Sune and then the hard part: tell my family that our Sunday was ruined.

They didn't take it well. Julie cried and said she missed me. My dad gave me one of those looks that strongly indicated I was not making the right choice. I felt bad for Julie, but I had to go. I promised her we would get ice cream when I got back. But I also knew it would probably never happen. I wouldn't be able to get back in time. Luckily for me, she forgot all about it when I told her that Tobias was coming because his dad, Sune, was going with me. So I got out of the house without anyone crying. Which was quite an accomplishment.

AT LEAST SUNE was in a great mood. Well, until I told him where we were going, that is. Then his smile froze and he looked mad.

"I didn't choose the location," I defended myself, thinking he was mad because it was so far away and he wouldn't get to spend any more of the Sunday with Tobias.

Sune stepped angrily on the gas pedal and we drove off.

"So, what happened?" he asked a little later with a less angry attitude.

"Some priest was killed in a juvenile prison."

He looked at me with worry in his eyes.

"What juvenile prison?"

"Stevnsfortet."

Sune was quiet for a while.

"What's wrong?" I asked after some time. We were almost there and I could see the prison on the top of the hill. I looked at Sune's face. He looked scared, as if something he just saw had frightened him. He didn't answer my question. Instead, he stopped the car in front of the crime tape. We got out.

A lot of people had gathered outside the prison, but no journalists just yet...mostly police officers discussing things and forensic people working. An officer talked to some of the employees, taking their statements. The blue van from Copenhagen was there again. This had to be big stuff.

Sune started taking pictures without saying a word to me, while I tried to contact some of the employees who had already given their statements.

I spotted a cleaning lady still wearing her uniform as she was about to walk away. Her head was bowed and she was crying. She passed the crime tape and I caught up with her.

"Do you know what happened?" I asked.

She stopped and stared at me with a frightened look.

"Hi, I'm Rebekka Franck with *Zeeland Times*," I said and gave her my card. "Would you mind making a statement for the newspaper?"

She sniffed and dried her eyes with the back of her hands. "Sure."

"Great." I found a new page in my notebook. "Tell me what you know."

"Someone killed the prison pastor."

I nodded and wrote it down. "Do you know his name?"

"Pastor Bertel...we called him...his last name was Lauritzen."

I stopped and looked at her. I remembered the name from the picture where Irene had written the names of the boys who raped her. I found the photo in my pocket and read the name out loud.

"Bertel Due-Lauritzen?" I showed her the picture and she pointed at one of the boys in the middle. Right behind Irene. Next to the handsome Bjorn Clausen.

"Yes, it was him."

"Do you know what happened to him?"

She shook her head heavily. "No. We found him on the floor in the church when we came to clean as we always do after Sunday service."

I wrote the details in my notebook.

"Could you tell what had killed him?"

She shook her head and started crying again. "No. It was like...he was...there was blood everywhere. And his chest was ripped...like if a beast had...and he was nailed to the floor."

"Nailed?"

"Yes, a big cross had gone through his head. Through his skull," she said, and put a finger to her head.

"It must have been a sharp cross?"

"I don't know about that."

"Of course you don't." I figured I would need to ask Sune one more time to get the autopsy report. I couldn't figure out how a cross could go through a skull.

"The man who did this is not human," the woman said. "He can't be."

She was the second one to tell me that and I was beginning to think she was right.

SUNE WAS STILL moody when we got back to the newspaper. He downloaded the pictures to the computer, while I wrote the article about the third killing. I spoke to the police shortly after I talked to the cleaning lady, but they had no comment, as I predicted. And, as earlier, they wouldn't say if they considered it to be the same killer.

The question in my mind was: Did Denmark have its first serial killer? There was no doubt in my mind that we did. So far, he had killed three out of the six people in the picture I had gotten from Irene. A fourth person had supposedly killed himself. Could it be Gyldenlove who killed the others? Or could it be Irene getting her revenge from the rape so many years ago? Or maybe it was a third person seeking revenge for something the gang did back then. Or maybe the last guy from the picture I had yet to meet? What was his name? I looked at the back of the picture. Christian Junge-Larsen. Maybe it was about time that I paid him a visit.

Sune got up from his seat and was about to leave when I stopped him.

"I need you to do something for me," I said.

"It's Sunday. It's going to cost you. I get paid by the hour, you know. Weekends cost extra."

"Actually, it's going to cost the newspaper, but they won't mind, since we're getting a lot of new readers because of this case."

He sat down at his desk. "So what do you want from me?"

"First, I need you to find Christian Junge-Larsen for me...his address and where he works. Next, I want more details on the killing of the prison pastor. The autopsy report is not going to be ready until at least tomorrow, so we can't find that. But I am interested in knowing more about the cross. By now, the officers must have made at least a report of the killing and a description of the crime scene. Could you try to find that?"

"Sure."

I got up and poured both of us a cup of coffee. I placed his in front of him. He didn't even look at me.

"The kids are having a blast at my dad's," I said. "So don't worry."

Sune looked at me and smiled for the first time in hours. "I know they're fine." His eyes went back to the screen.

"So what's the matter?"

He sighed. "Nothing. Just a little personal stuff. Could we leave it at that?"

I nodded and looked out the window. It was still Sunday and the town of Karrebaeksminde was sleepy. People stayed indoors, where they could keep warm. Watching TV, playing cards or board games, and just relaxing and getting new energy for the next week of work. The streets were empty. I only saw an elderly man walking his dog. And all of a sudden, it struck me. Wasn't it my duty as a reporter to tell people the truth? I had kept my knowledge hidden from them. Out there in the normally quiet little kingdom was a killer on the loose. It wasn't three random killings, as the police had told the public and wanted me to write in the newspaper...like they had said to all the other reporters. They didn't want to scare the public, yes, I knew that. But it was wrong. People were entitled to know the truth. That we did, in fact, have a serial killer. A seriously dangerous beast.

I sat down at my desk and made my decision. I was going to write the truth for the morning paper. I was going to tell the public that the three killings were related. That the victims had all known each other at the boarding school.

22

"The cross looks like it was made of big iron spikes," Sune said after a while. I had just begun my new article and it was coming along nicely.

"Take a look," he said, and pointed at the screen.

I stood and went to his desk. I looked over his shoulder and saw a picture taken at the scene.

"It looks like it was welded," I said and pointed.

"Yes, it looks very homemade."

"Like someone took two spikes and welded them together to make it look like a real cross."

"Exactly."

"And the spikes are sharp on the end, so they could easily penetrate the skull," I said, thinking now all we had to do was to figure out who would have spikes like these at their disposal. Maybe the killer worked with this kind of thing.

"So what do you think?" I asked Sune.

He shook his head. "I really don't know."

"A welder?"

"Or someone who builds houses?" he suggested.

I nodded. That was a good idea. This kind of spike could be used to keep panels or planks together. But the killer would also know how to weld. So they were looking for a craftsman or a contractor of some kind. Not a nobleman like Gyldenlove and probably not a woman like Irene.

"There was something else," Sune said.

"Yes?"

"I got a little more information on Bjorn Clausen, the guy who killed himself in 1987."

I looked with interest at him.

"Well, according to the school archives, he was at the school on a scholarship. It's not something the boarding school normally does, but his mother apparently knew the headmaster."

"How do you know that?"

"I talked to him."

"The headmaster?"

"Yes, I visited him. He's in a nursing home now. Waiting to die. Sick from some sort of cancer. Anyway, he felt like confiding in me, and since his wife passed away a long time ago, he said he thought it was about time to tell someone."

"I can't believe you visited him without telling me."

"I did it Friday after work. I thought it was a long shot, since he was probably senile, but he wasn't."

"So what did he tell you?"

"That he had an affair with Bjorn Clausen's mother. It lasted several years. He loved her and he believed he might have been the father of her sons. But she rejected that idea and he never did know if they were his kids."

"Wow. That's brutal."

"I know. But he told me that he let Bjorn and his younger brother in on a scholarship. It was a fictional scholarship, though. He made it up and paid for the boys out of his own pocket. He wanted them to have the very best education they could get without anyone knowing the truth."

"So Bjorn was a local boy who got accepted into the fine company of the noble?"

"Precisely."

"But that doesn't explain why he killed himself."

"No. If he killed himself," Sune said.

I looked at him. We had discussed it earlier. Both of us couldn't quite get rid of the thought that maybe Bjorn Clausen was the killer's first victim back in 1987.

"What are you saying?"

He shook his head again. "I don't know."

"You must have some idea or you wouldn't say that. I know that much about you."

"It's just that...It's probably nothing." Sune hesitated.

"What? You're killing me here."

"Well, it's about the report the police made back then. The conductor's statement was a little strange, I think."

"Why?"

Sune clicked the mouse a few times with his hand which only had three fingers and found some documents he showed me.

"Look. In the first statement made on the scene, the conductor of the train says that Bjorn Clausen was already lying on the ground on the tracks when he hit him with the train. But in the second one, he states that Bjorn fell from the bridge as the train came by and he hit him while he was in the air. And if you look at where the body hit the train, Bjorn was pulled under the train. The body didn't hit the train on the way down from the bridge."

"It was already on the tracks, like he said in the first statement."

We were both quiet for a moment. We didn't know exactly what this meant.

"I just know that if I was going to kill myself by jumping in front of a train," Sune said, "I would make sure to hit the train at full speed while in the air so I would die quickly."

"Well, maybe he miscalculated. Maybe he jumped too soon and hit the tracks first and then the train arrived."

"That's possible. As I said, I don't know. I just found it odd."

"It is odd and I don't believe in coincidences. Either Bjorn Clausen was killed by the same killer who is murdering right now or he killed himself because of all the things they did back then. That's my theory. I don't know if we will ever find out."

AS WE SAT THERE TALKING QUIETLY, we sensed something was wrong. We couldn't put a finger on what it was until the editorial room suddenly was filled with police officers. Men in uniform approached Sune. I got up.

"What the hell are you doing here?"

A voice answered from the doorway. I looked and saw Michael Oestergaard.

He too approached Sune.

"Sune Johanssen?"

Sune looked at me and I felt a shiver. It was my fault for pushing him into hacking again. Oh, my God. What had I done?

"You are under arrest for the murder of Pastor Bertel Due-Lauritzen earlier today."

My eyes widened. What?

"Are you kidding me? He was with me all day."

Detective Oestergaard looked at me. "Was he with you between 10:45 and 11:30 this morning?"

I went silent. We hadn't met until three.

"But there is no way..."

The detective stopped me.

"As I said earlier this week, let us do the police work."

I was so mad I could have punched him. But I kept my calm and quieted down. While they took Sune away, I yelled that I would take care of Tobias and help him get out.

"Whatever it takes," I said, but I wasn't so sure of anything anymore.

23

It was Sunday night so there really wasn't much I could do to help Sune until the morning. So I finished my article and sent it to my editor, who loved it.

"This will sell a lot of newspapers," he responded.

But it didn't make me happy at all. Nothing could. I didn't understand a thing. How could the police think that Sune had anything to do with the murder of that priest? He could never do a thing like that. Had everybody lost their minds overnight?

I went home, promising myself that I would get Sune the best lawyer in the country once I woke up. I had some money put away and could afford to help him.

The kids were in bed but not yet asleep when I got home, so I got to tuck them in. I love doing that. My dad had put an extra mattress on the floor in Julie's room. They were both smiling widely when I came in.

"We're having a sleepover," Julie said.

"I know," I said and smiled.

Tobias laughed. "I wanna do this every day," he said, and then Julie laughed too.

Well that just might have to be the case, if they keep Sune, I thought. It was a good thing the two kids loved each other.

I read them a couple of books and finally they both fell asleep. Julie was holding Tobias' hand. As they both dozed off, their hands slowly slipped out of their grip.

I kissed my dad goodnight and he went to bed after a tiring day of taking care of the kids.

So I was alone. Not something I had been good at lately. I felt sad and sorry for Sune. I didn't know what was going on or how to undo it. I had to try to visit him tomorrow if he wasn't released by then. They couldn't keep him for more than twenty-four hours without him seeing a judge. And, by tomorrow, they would know they had made a mistake. Of course they would. Sune couldn't kill anyone. That was impossible.

I made myself some tea and sat in my dad's favorite chair. No TV, no kids, no anything. Just me and my hot cup of tea. I looked out into the dark and was thinking about Giovanni when the phone rang.

"That didn't last long," I murmured, but then I saw that it was him.

"Just the person I was thinking of," I said as I answered.

IT DIDN'T TAKE him much effort to convince me to leave my tea and come to his beach house. He said he wanted to see me. He missed me, and that was all I had to hear. I really needed someone to talk to right now. Someone who would listen and understand my frustration. And Giovanni was the best listener.

HE SMILED his bright smile when he opened the door and let me in. Always the gentleman, he took my jacket and poured me a glass of red wine.

"Only one," I said. "I have to get back to the kids tonight so my dad won't be alone with two."

Giovanni looked surprised at me.

"Two kids? Did you have another one since we last saw each other?"

I laughed. It felt good. Then I told him the whole story about Sune and the murder they apparently thought he had committed.

Giovanni listened as always and looked serious while I spoke.

"So you don't think he could have done it?" he said.

"There is no way!"

"Hmm..."

"What?"

"Nothing."

"You can't be serious!"

"It's just..."

"What?"

"Well the police arrested him. They must have something, some kind of evidence. You told me he's already been in prison."

"In juvenile prison. For hacking. Not for killing anyone or even hurting anyone."

"How long have you known him?"

"Only about a week."

He drank his wine and looked at me. I knew what he was saying, but I couldn't believe it. I didn't want to.

"Face it. You don't know anything about the guy."

"I just know he couldn't do it."

Now it was my turn to drink. I stared out the panoramic window. The ocean was calmer tonight, but we could still hear the waves as they rolled in on the beach. I loved that sound.

"What about the other killings?" I asked.

"What do you mean?"

"Well, all the victims have a connection. They all went to the same school together. They were friends."

"So?"

"So, could Sune have killed the others too?"

I thought it through. Was it really possible for Sune to have committed these killings? When I first met him, it was at Didrik Rosenfeldt's summer residence. The first murder had already taken place. Sune could have done it the night before. I had no way of knowing.

The next one was Henrik Holch. Sune was with me when we heard about it. But the murder had been committed the night before and I wasn't with him then. And the last one? The priest? Was it really possible that he could have driven to Roedvig Stevns, an hour away, killed the priest, then come back to Karrebaeksminde and gone with me in the afternoon? It was possible. But not likely. Not to me. And what about Bjorn Clausen who was killed in 1987? Sune was hardly born then, so that was out of the question. But, then again, it might have been a real suicide. I had no argument, no alibis to support his innocence. I just knew in my heart that he was innocent. "I just have a gut feeling about this guy, that's all." I finished my glass of red wine and got up.

"I need to go to the bathroom." I was about to go upstairs when Giovanni grabbed my hand and pulled me near him. He put his arm around me and started kissing me on the neck. I felt a nice shiver all the way down my back. Then I felt his warm breath in my ear. His muscular body came closer to mine. His lips were warm and soft as they touched mine.

I stopped him. "I really have to go to the bathroom," I said, laughing like a little girl.

He smiled and let me go.

"The one upstairs is clogged. Use the one in the back."

THE TOILET in the back was right next to the studio where Giovanni made his sculptures. I had to go through the studio to get to the bathroom. I had never been in there before and I was quite curious to see it. So, after my visit to the toilet, I found myself in the middle of a totally different world. This was where the magic was made.

I looked at one of the sculptures he was working on and tried to imagine what it would look like when it was done. And how did an artist like Giovanni even know when it was done? If it was anything like writing, then you could always find something, some little thing that could have been better. I knew about that from the book I wrote about my trip to Iraq. It didn't make me a millionaire, but it was fun to write something for once that wasn't thrown away a few hours later and forgotten. It was something I had created, something my kid would have and read long after I was gone.

The sculpture in front of me seemed to be mocking me. The look in his eyes was strange and scary. I kept staring into his eyes for a while, and when I moved my head, my eyes caught something. On a bench right beside the sculpture was a hammer and a chisel. I took the chisel in my hand. It was heavy. I touched the pointy part at one end. It looked exactly like the welded spikes in the photo.

I put it down and looked around. At the other end of the studio, I saw something else. I went there and my heart started pounding in my chest when I realized what it was.

It was a welding machine.

On a table, I saw heavy leather gloves and a protective long-sleeved jacket to avoid exposure to the extreme heat and flames.

"The brightness of the welding area can lead to a condition called arc eye, in which ultraviolet light causes inflammation of the cornea and can burn the retinas of the eyes," a voice said behind me.

I turned around. Giovanni had come into the studio. He took up a mask and put it on so it covered his face.

"Goggles and welding helmets with dark face plates prevent this exposure," he continued, while picking up another mask and putting it on. "And, in recent years, new helmet models have been produced that feature a face plate that automatically darkens upon exposure to high amounts of UV light."

He threw the mask on the table, took a step to the right, and pulled out a curtain.

"To protect bystanders, I put up opaque welding curtains to surround the welding area. These curtains, made of a polyvinyl chloride plastic film, shield any spectators from exposure to the UV light from the electric arc."

I nodded. "A lot of security is needed." I took a few steps away from him.

Then I felt him grab me around the waist. He pulled me close. My heart beat faster.

"You are so beautiful, do you know that?" he asked.

I forced a smile. I tried to hear over my heart racing in my chest. I didn't know what to think. And I had a hard time thinking at all. I really liked the guy, but the fact was that I didn't know anything about him.

Giovanni lifted me up and cleared a table behind us. He put me down on the table and leaned on me. I felt a hand under my skirt. He was breathing heavily when he aggressively removed my panties in one move.

"You bring out the beast in me!" he groaned, with what felt like explosive rage.

THE SEX in the studio was intense, to put it mildly. Giovanni was wild as an animal and revealed a side I hadn't seen before in him. Or in me. It was crazy, not like anything I had experienced. And I hate to admit it, but I liked it in a way. The thing is, I couldn't really figure out if it was the sex itself or the tiny bit of fear of what he would do to me that made it so...scintillating. At one point, he even grabbed my neck with both of his hands, and I was afraid that he would strangle me. But then he let go.

Afterwards, we tumbled into the living room and threw ourselves on the pillows on the floor in front of the fireplace, where Giovanni lit the fire. We both groaned, breathing heavily. He poured us another glass of wine, and I thought that after all that exercise I must have already burned off the first one. So I took it and drank it. I felt lightheaded.

"So you've never told me anything about yourself." I looked down at him with his head in my lap.

He smiled. "Why is it that women always want to talk about stuff like that after sex?"

"I don't know. Because we want to know who we just slept with? Whether we should regret it or do it again?"

He laughed and looked into the fire. But he didn't answer me.

"So where are you from?"

"Like that's any secret to you."

"I know you are originally from Milan, but why did you come to Denmark?"

"My father is Danish. I came here when I was fifteen. He got a job in Copenhagen. So we moved here."

"So that's where you got those blue eyes," I said.

He nodded and sat up.

"So where did you go to school? You must have been in ninth grade back then." I drank my wine, trying to pretend like the question wasn't important. Trying to act casual.

Again, he avoided answering. Instead, he took the glass out of my hand and kissed me.

Then he whispered, "What's with all the questions? What does it really matter where we come from and what we did before we met? What is important right now is that we are together. Nothing else really matters when it comes to love."

I smiled. He was so smooth.

"Did you go to boarding school?"

It was a reasonable question, since a lot of children who came to Denmark from foreign countries and didn't speak the language went to Herlufsholm boarding school, where they had a special program for international kids.

Giovanni sighed and got up from the floor.

"Now I'll get us something to eat. I made Ricotta e cioccolato. You know, like a chocolate pie."

I went home with a strange feeling inside of me. I couldn't escape the facts. Giovanni had a welding machine, not something everybody had. On top of that, he had spikes lying around. And he was about the same age as the victims. He could easily have been a student at the same school...something he apparently didn't want to tell me.

Why all the secrecy if he had nothing to hide?

24

The next morning, I went to visit Sune after dropping off the kids at school. I had talked to Sara and asked her to get ahold of the best lawyer money could buy.

Sune looked exhausted. His green Mohawk was flaccid, his eyes red, and his skin paler than the dingy white wall behind him. I felt so sorry for him. The police would only let me talk to him for a minute, so I had to be brief. A police officer listened in from the corner of the small room.

I grabbed his hand.

"No touching," the officer said.

I moved my hand. "Sorry," I said to the officer.

I looked back at Sune. "How are you?" He sighed.

"That bad?"

"All this is just because I was in that stupid juvenile prison. Only because my friend didn't think when he hacked into the files of PET. He was stupid and left traces. And that led them straight to me."

"You hacked The Police Intelligence?" I couldn't help myself. I was impressed with him. He had only been a teenager back then.

"Yes, first I did, and then I showed my friend how to do it. I never should have done that. It's always easy to be smart in hindsight, right?"

I nodded. I had done that a lot of times in my life...regretted decisions, trusted the wrong people.

"Is Stevnsfortet the prison you went to?"

"Yes."

So that was his connection to the pastor.

"And it was still the same pastor, I'm guessing. But why would anyone think that you killed the pastor just because you were in there a long time ago?"

"Because I could have done it."

I widened my eyes and didn't know quite what to believe anymore.

"What are you saying?"

"I wanted that guy dead as much as anyone else who had ever been to that prison."

I'd never seen this kind of anger in that gentle guy. It was very unusual.

"Why?"

He held his hand up and showed me the two missing fingers. "Because he did this," he said.

"What? The pastor?" I could not believe what I was hearing.

"Yes."

"I don't get it. Why would a pastor do that to you?"

"That's what he did to a lot of us."

"Cut off your fingers?"

"Cut anything off that had to do with the crime we were in for."

"So he took your fingers because you used them for hacking?"

"Yes, and he castrated those who were in for rape, and so on."

I leaned back in my chair, astonished that a thing like that could go on in a Danish prison without anyone knowing.

"But why wasn't he stopped a long time ago?"

"No one dares to tell. There's a story about one boy who tried to tell, but no one believed him, and the following night he got his tongue cut out. So he couldn't talk anymore."

"Wow. That is a horrible story. But who did the prison guards think it was then? I mean, the evidence is pretty obvious."

"They thought it was something going on among ourselves, the prisoners. Like personal, drug related or hierarchy stuff, and they didn't really care. They would just put us in the hospital and then back in the cell when we had been treated."

"And he has been doing this for all these years to all the prisoners?"

"Well, it wasn't all the prisoners he would do this to. Just a few of us who he thought needed more punishment, I guess. Those who did the same crime more than once or the ones who claimed themselves to be innocent. Those who wouldn't repent."

"Like you."

"Like me."

"But that doesn't quite explain why they think you killed him. It could have been any one of the prisoners who wanted revenge."

"Yeah, well, I threatened him. I was so mad back then that I said in front of everybody in the prison, including the warden, that I would hunt him down and put one of his crosses through his skull."

"Oh."

"Yeah, I kind of dug my own grave there."

That really wasn't good. Sune had an excellent motive and he had even told how he would do it.

"But I didn't do it," he said.

I looked at him and believed him.

"I don't have it in me to kill someone. I just know I couldn't do it. And now they are accusing me of having planned it all in the last couple of years. They even think that's why I moved down here."

"What else are they saying?"

"That I came in after the Sunday morning service and killed the pastor in the confession chair in the prison church."

"But don't they keep records of who visits the prison?"

"Sure they do, but they think I either paid someone off to let me in or that I know the area so well I somehow knew a way to sneak inside."

"That sounds like a weak theory."

"That's what they're trying to get me to tell them. How I got in.

Apparently, someone did visit the prison that morning. Under the name Bjorn Clausen."

"You're kidding me. But he's dead, right?"

"I know. But they think I might have used a false name. You know, it is a juvenile prison. That means they like to call it an institution. Most of the inmates are allowed to have visitors and their names are registered in the computers, but not checked or cleared. With a fake ID, anyone could get in under a false name."

I opened my mouth and was about to ask another question when the officer interrupted us.

"Time is up," he said.

Two officers came into the room and grabbed Sune by the arms.

"I'll get you the best lawyer; I promise you that," I said to him. "I'll get you out of here in no time. You'll see Tobias soon."

I looked him in the eyes just in time to see a little sparkle of hope in them, and then he left the room between the two officers.

On my way home, I felt the anger rage inside of me. Didn't they see the connection between the killings at all? It was so obvious to me, but it was like the police didn't want to see it. Were they really that stupid and incompetent? I normally wouldn't believe that about our police force, but this made me think that there was only one way out for Sune.

I had to catch the killer myself.

25

Back at the office, Sara was talking on the phone. She tried her best to convince one lawyer after another that they needed to help Sune. She guaranteed the bill would be paid and they were sure to win the case, since he was not guilty.

But still she had no luck. They were all too busy or they didn't care much for a small case like that, and they certainly didn't want to lose.

"What about just helping someone in need?" I heard her yell at one point and then slam the phone down.

My editor was in a better mood. He called me and said he loved my article on the boarding school connection and wanted to do more about the serial killer angle.

"And no one has complained?" I asked.

"About the article? Of course. There's always someone who complains," he said. "But that won't stop us."

I was beginning to love my new editor. Nothing seemed to put him down.

"So, who was it? Rosenfeldt? The police?"

"Ah, well, if you must know, both of them."

"And you're not having second thoughts?"

"That someone this important is complaining just shows me that we are on to something really big and that's what it's all about. That's why we hired you and pay you three times as much as the rest of our staff."

I was proud. My new editor had a way of making me feel like I was the most important reporter on the newspaper. And he said any trouble that headed my way he would gladly take care of.

"What about Sune?" I asked.

"The newspaper can't do much for him. It's a personal matter. But I'm very happy to hear you and Sara are working on getting him a lawyer."

I looked at my co-worker, who waved her arms around like windmill while talking firmly to the person on the other end of the phone.

"Keep me posted on what's going on with him; we stick together at this paper. We help each other," he said before he hung up.

I looked at Sara, who now gave me two thumbs up.

"We got one," she said and hung up. "A really good one, too."

I took in a deep breath. I was so relieved.

"Good job."

MEANWHILE, I had an idea for how we should pursue the serial killer angle. When I was in Iraq I got to know an American named James Wickham, who worked at the base as a psychologist for soldiers in crisis. I knew that he had gotten a job at the FBI to work as a profiling expert. Over the years, he became an expert in serial killers and how their brains worked. I had used him previously for another article about the condition of the soldiers when they returned from war. That's when he told me about his new job. They knew a lot more about serial killers in the U.S. than we did, so I thought he might teach me something about them.

I called him at his office in Washington, D.C.

"Rebekka Franck? I never thought I would hear that beautiful voice again."

I loved Americans. They were always so positive and always gave compliments. Very different from the Danish Jantelov, as we called it, most popularly described as the belief that people shouldn't think they are somebody, because they're not. It was a way of thinking that often kept us from complimenting others and led to low self-esteem. It was a way of thinking that we Danes had a hard time escaping.

"Well, you did," I said, blushing.

"What can I do for you?"

"I think we might have a serial killer on the loose."

"In Denmark? I can't believe it. Well it's about time you guys grew up, right?" He laughed.

"You might be right. The thing is, we have very little experience with how this type of killer thinks or acts. The reason for calling you today is I want to do an article about serial killers."

"Oh, okay. That shouldn't be too hard. I mean, no two killers are alike, but there are the general characteristics on how they think and such. I can certainly help you with that."

"Thanks."

"First, I would like to give you a short definition of a serial killer as we use it here at the FBI. According to our definition, a serial murder is the unlawful killing of two or more victims by the same offender or offenders, in separate events."

"We've got that. That's for sure," I said, leaving out that the police didn't think that it was the same offender. Not yet at least. Not until I could prove them wrong.

"Okay, what else can you tell me about the killings?"

I explained the case to him in detail and he was quiet for a little while afterwards.

"I see. So you have a killer who kills in the same way, by ripping his victims open, so to speak? And he has killed three people so far?"

"Yes, that's right. Also, all the victims know each other from the school. So what kind of a psychopath do we have here?"

"It sounds to me like what you have here is a very organized offender. Everything is planned to perfection. He leaves no trace of committing the crime and he generally kills by the same methods. Generally, the organized offender commits well-planned and well-orchestrated offenses, whereas the disorganized offender commits more poorly planned and poorly executed offenses."

"What does that tell us about him?"

"The more organization demonstrated by an offender, the more likely the offender will be intelligent, socially competent, capable of skilled employment, conscious of evidence, controlled, and able to avoid identification while accounting for a greater number of victims. They lack feelings of guilt or remorse and view their victims as mere objects that they can manipulate for their own perverse satisfaction and sense of power, control, mastery, and domination. Organized serial murderers may kill in such great numbers due to fantasies that feed their predatory desires and lead them to compete with themselves in a perverted contest of 'practice makes perfect.' In other words, they continue to kill, in part, due to a desire to improve upon their last murder. In addition, they understand their misbehavior, know the difference between right and wrong, and can choose when and where to act upon their urges."

"So who is he? What kind of person are we talking about?"

"On television and the silver screen, serial killers are usually white males and dysfunctional loners who really want to get caught. Or, they're super-intelligent monsters who frustrate law enforcement at every turn. That's not the case, though. Serial killers are not all dysfunctional loners. Some have wives and kids and full-time jobs and are active in their community or church or both. This man lives in your midst as a normal person. He does things that normal people do. He goes to the bar to have a drink. He goes to restaurants the same as we all do. Nothing in his everyday behavior will indicate that he is killing people."

I wrote in my notebook while the thoughts of Giovanni kept messing with my mind. He seemed perfectly normal. He was intelligent and very good at manipulating. He seemed like a fit for the profile. But, then again, so did Sune.

"So what kind of a person becomes a serial killer? Someone who has experienced childhood abuse?" I asked.

"Many individuals have experienced childhood abuse, and the

vast majority don't become criminals, much less serial murderers. Most abused children adjust and, as they mature, progress past their traumatic experiences. However, those individuals who become serial murderers do not adjust or put the trauma and its influence in the past. They ruminate about their mistreatment, dwell on their past experiences, and become frustrated, angry, and depressed."

"Is he a psychopath?"

"The relationship between psychopathic and serial killers is particularly interesting. All psychopaths do not become serial murderers. Lucky for us, because there are a lot of them out there. But serial murderers may possess some or many of the traits consistent with those of a psychopath. Psychopaths who commit serial murder do not value human life and are extremely callous in their interactions with their victims. This is particularly evident in sexually motivated serial killers who repeatedly target, stalk, assault, and kill without a sense of remorse. However, being a psychopath alone does not explain the motivations of a serial killer. Psychopaths are not sensitive to themes such as sympathy for their victims or remorse or guilt over their crimes. They do possess certain personality traits that can be detected, particularly their inherent narcissism, selfishness, and vanity. Psychopathy is a personality disorder manifested in people who use a mixture of charm, manipulation, intimidation, and occasionally violence to control others, in order to satisfy their own selfish needs."

I had to take a deep breath to calm down. All he said fit perfectly with Giovanni. The narcissism, the vanity, the manipulation, and the selfish needs.

James continued, "If a violent offender is psychopathic, he's able to assault, rape, and murder without concern for legal, moral, or social consequences. This allows him to do what he wants, whenever he wants. The way he kills is an indication of who he is. It's clearly a ritual to him and has a special meaning to him, though we don't know what the meaning is. He knows the meaning and maybe his victims do too."

"So how do we stop him?"

"Unlike what they say in the movies, the serial killer does not want to get caught. Over time, as he kills without being discovered, he will get careless during his crimes."

"So what you are basically telling me is that we have to wait for him to make a mistake?"

"That's exactly what I'm saying."

I WROTE the article and found a nice picture on the Internet of my American friend to put next to the story. Then I pressed the "send" button and mailed it to my editor. I leaned back, satisfied with myself. I had left one part out of the article, though, something James told me just before we hung up. A serial killer often had a "cooling off period." Often he would commit his first murder and then have a long period maybe of ten or more years before he would kill again. That substantiated my theory that Bjorn Clausen didn't commit suicide but was killed by the same perpetrator. But I had no documentation to prove it. So I left it out of the article.

But I still kept thinking about Sune. In my book, there was no way he could be the killer. He was only three years old in 1987. But as long as the police didn't recognize the connections between the killings, that argument would do him no good.

I sighed and looked at Sara. She had gone back to listening to the police scanner again while she typed on her laptop. She had a half-eaten piece of cake on her desk.

Then I looked back at my own desk and my eyes caught a little yellow sticky note that Sune must have put there some time before he was arrested.

It was the address of Christian Junge-Larsen.

The last guy in the picture.

26

C hristian Junge-Larsen looked at himself in the mirror.

"My God, I look like I could be dead."

Not that it was that big of a surprise to him, since he hadn't slept in days. He didn't even know what time it was any longer, whether day or night outside Marienlyst Casino. He remembered this morning he went home to his apartment in Elsinore—the famous city of Shakespeare's Hamlet—and got a few hours of sleep. Dead drunk, he collapsed on the bed. But it didn't erase the circles under his eyes or give him the color back in his face. He looked like he hadn't seen the sun in days, which he actually hadn't. The dimmed light in the bathroom of the fancy casino was kind to him, he knew. He looked much worse in real light.

He splashed some water on his face and washed it with the casino's hand soap. It smelled like lemons, and with that, he thought he was ready for another couple of hours by the blackjack table or at the roulette wheel. The casino wouldn't close until four in the morning.

He went out and sat with the other men just like him. Men with a feverish look...with eyes that wouldn't let go of the ball going around the wheel. Christian Junge-Larsen put everything on red nine, knowing deep down inside himself that he was about to pave another mile of his road straight to hell.

He saw the wheel spin and the ball jump and dance around and, like so many times before, he didn't win. The croupier mechanically swept his bets off the table with that same professional look every croupier had. The look didn't change even if a player sobbed and cried and told him that this was his life savings, his last money. The same look that didn't distinguish between a hundred-dollar win and a million.

Things had gotten really bad over the last couple of months. He had lost everything, including his lucrative job as CEO of the company his father had built. Over a period of five years, he had stolen about ten million dollars from the company without them knowing it. But over the years, he had gotten too careless, and one day he got caught. Because it was his father's company, they didn't turn him over to the police, but they threw him out instead.

Maybe he would have been better off in prison, he often thought to himself.

The big mansion on the water was next to go, then the car, and finally the wife and the kids left. Now he lived alone in an apartment where he hadn't paid the rent in two months. No housekeeper, no gardener, and no chauffeur. It was just him and his own damn mess.

Fuck them, he thought. Everything was about to change. It had to. He just needed to get his luck back. Then maybe one day he would get his beloved wife back too. She had tried to stand by him, but it was like living with a drug addict. He would promise he would stop, that this time was the last time. And then he would stay away from the casino for a couple of days until he felt the urge again, that alluring and deceitful feeling that this time he could actually have a win, that it was possible. He knew it was, because in the beginning he had won several times. And he always would win a little when he first sat down at the table. He would also lose a little, but mostly win. And then he wouldn't know how to stop. He always just needed one more try...and then he would lose. Then one more and he would eventually lose it all. That was his curse.

And so it went this night, just like every other night. He lost, and by four o'clock in the morning he would leave the casino drunk and out of money. The worst part was he knew the casino wouldn't open again until six in the evening the next day.

He had to walk home. He was cold in his white shirt and black Armani jacket he always wore when he went to gamble. Once he used to own hundreds of suits like this. But now he only had the one left. He kept it clean and nice so it would always make him look like he still had a lot of money. Otherwise, they wouldn't let him into the casino.

He had borrowed some money from his brother, who had complained a lot, but eventually given him ten thousand dollars to get back on his feet again. Then he had told Christian he had reached his limit. The money would have been enough to pay his rent and patch up a number of critical emergencies with his financial situation—like paying off that scumbag Brian who kept stalking him for the money he borrowed six months ago and kept threatening to send a couple of Hell's Angels rockers after him. But Christian never paid off his debt with the money from his brother. Instead, he spent it in the casino, under the excuse that he was attempting to make more.

But his fate was always to see others strike gold. He never failed to be there if someone got one of the big wins...the ones they all were longing so desperately for. The kind which just might have hit him instead, if only he had been at the right place at the right time.

It started to rain just as Christian reached his apartment lobby. He got inside just in time. Maybe he hadn't totally run out of luck, after all.

Inside the apartment, he sat down on his bed. He looked around. He still couldn't believe that he lived like this. He, who grew up never having to do anything by himself. He, who had gotten a Porsche when he turned eighteen, when he could get his license in Denmark. He, who was friends with some of the richest and most influential people in the country, or at least he used to be. He, who used to be the one bossing people around, telling them what to do. He, who used to have people's respect just because of who he was, just because of his name.

"Forty-six years old," he murmured, while he rested his exhausted body on the bed. "I might as well be dead."

27

"Seven, eight, better stay up late..."

The voice whispering in Christian Junge-Larsen's left ear was gentle and familiar. He was still lying on the bed, fully clothed. He thought it was just a part of his dream. His breath was calm and peaceful. Then the voice was there again with that song. His dream suddenly changed. Indecipherable images agitated his sleep.

HE IS ALONE in a dark place. Then he hears voices, singing and laughing. Singing that same old song from the movies they used to watch at the boarding school when the lights were out and everybody was supposed to be asleep.

That is where he is, he figures. In one of the dorms. And these are the voices. He knows them. They have been haunting him.

All of a sudden, he sees a light and he walks towards it. It is a door that leads into another room. He opens the door and sees what he believes are his friends. He can't really see them or their faces. They stand in the middle of the room with their backs turned toward him. They are looking at something on the ground. Or is it someone?

He walks closer. Anxiety rises in him. He can hear his own heavy breath. His friends are hitting and kicking someone on the floor. The screams are horrible. He stops and wants to run away, and suddenly he is climbing stairs, running up and up while his friends are beneath him. Still laughing and singing, almost chanting. The stairs continue and seem like they will never end. A light shines at the top, but he doesn't seem to be able to ever reach it, no matter how hard he tries to climb the steps.

He looks down and feels like the stairs are floating in the air. The height makes him dizzy and he almost falls, but he gets his balance back just in time. The voices from beneath are getting louder and louder, as does the screaming and the sounds of the beating...the sound of fists hitting flesh, breaking bones, and crushing lives. The worst sound in the world.

Christian is running again. He climbs another step and tries to get away, to get to the top. Away from the laughing and beating and the screams. But every time he succeeds in climbing another step, three more appear at the top. Then four, then five. His breathing gets even heavier as he climbs reluctantly.

He sees the light at the end and runs even faster up the stairs. He sees a door at the end and reaches for the handle. He can almost feel it in his right hand as he tries to grab it. He can feel the warmth of the light behind the door that is about to greet him and give him the peace he so desperately needs.

But, instead, he slips and falls.

All the way back down the stairs. Hitting every step on the way that he had just climbed. Bruising his back and his head.

Why? Why? he keeps thinking.

And then he finds himself on the floor in the dorm. Surrounded by all of his friends. They are still singing and laughing, and now he knows why.

He is their victim. He is the one they are kicking and beating.

CHRISTIAN WOKE UP. His hand raised in the dark, reaching for the floor lamp. He turned it on and a dim light spread through the bare room.

The voice came at once from the man sitting in front of him.

"Today is a good day to die, don't you think?"

Christian got up from the bed and ran past the man sitting in the chair. Just like in the dream, he ran for his life, feeling the door handle, but never reaching it. Instead, he felt an arm grab him from behind, throw him onto the floor, and then he was kicked in the face. Christian opened his mouth to scream, but the man covered his mouth with his gloved hand and the sound leaving Christian's mouth was now more of surprise and fear.

WHEN THE KILLER slit his throat, a red spurt came out so fast it hit the yellow lampshade. Then the lifeless body of Christian Junge-Larsen slumped down onto the cheap carpet.

Then there was a noise on the stairs outside. Steps of a person approaching the apartment. As he cleaned the sharp blades of the glove on a jacket lying on the floor, the killer smiled again.

28

I had spent the rest of the Monday trying to reach the last guy in the picture, Christian Junge-Larsen, at his home in Elsinore, but apparently his phone was out of order and he apparently had no cell phone. Maybe Sune could have done a better job with his skills on the computer, but I was on my own for now. So I decided to go to Elsinore alone the next day.

I was sitting in my car on the highway when my phone rang again. I picked it up, but put it down after one quick look at it. It was Giovanni, again. He'd called me at least eight times the night before and this morning. I hadn't answered any of the calls. Why? Simply because I had no idea what to say to him. What could I say? That I thought he might be a vicious killer? Either that would be true and he certainly wouldn't tell me but maybe just get rid of me instead, or it was not true and then that would probably be the end of our relationship. With trust issues like that, I would be sure to scare any man off.

I wasn't sure of anything right now, and I really liked the guy, so I was determined to stay away from him until everything was solved. I had to know the truth and I had to find it myself.

My hope was that Christian Junge-Larsen had some answers that could help me.

. . .

I PARKED on the street in front of the address that Sune had found. It was still pretty early. I had left at six in the morning to get there and catch him before he went to work. The city was quiet but awake. People bicycled to work or school; some waited for the bus at the stop close to the building that Christian Junge-Larsen lived in. Kids with their big schoolbags passed me. They were wearing big jackets and winter hats. When I got out of the car, I spotted Kronborg in the background, the castle where the Prince of Denmark in *Hamlet* discovers that his father—the king—did not die a natural death, and later on finds out his own brother, the new king of Denmark, killed him.

Even back then, crime mysteries interested people, I thought to myself, while staring at the red brick castle with the green oxidized-copper roof. It was beautiful, standing there with the ocean surrounding it.

From my history classes, I remembered in the basement was a big statue of an old legend named Holger Danske. The myth went that whenever the kingdom was threatened by an enemy from the outside, the stone statue would become flesh and bone and Holger Danske would emerge and defend his country.

I liked those kinds of stories and, for some reason, I remembered them.

It was a really cold morning. The sun shone, but the wind was freezing and going right through my jacket. I hurried into the building and found the stairs.

There was no name on the door, but I rang the bell anyway, hoping Christian Junge-Larsen was still living there. I was really surprised that a man of his status would live in a dump like this. I had googled him before I went there and he had been quite the big-shot for a lot of years, living the high-class jet-set life and marrying some Czech super-model with cheekbones that went straight up under both ears, and legs as long as most of my whole body. It was, of course, his parents who had started the company and made their name big. All Christian Junge-Larsen had to do—after finishing boarding school and his business education in London—was to run the family company as the CEO and live the sweet life that his parents worked their butts off to give him.

But, for some reason, he was fired by the company's board some years ago, and he then seemed to have vanished into thin air after that. I had found his model wife and the kids living at another address now, so I figured they had separated.

No one answered when I rang the doorbell, so I tried knocking instead, but as I did, the door came open. I took a step back. I didn't want to intrude. But then curiosity got the better of me and I gently pushed the door a little more until it was half open.

A second later I wished I had never done so.

I FELT my blood turn to ice. I had to force myself to breathe deeply. A trail of blood continued along the floor and disappeared through an open door. As I walked into the apartment, I was hit by the sweetish smell of blood.

I don't know why I didn't turn around and run at that point, but something urged me to follow the trail of blood into the next room of the apartment. It was a messy place—clothing all over the floor, mixed with old beer bottles and half-empty pizza boxes.

When I got to the door of the next room and could see inside, I felt the ice spreading throughout my body. Lying on the bed was the body of a man. His throat was ripped open by what looked like four knives.

"Or the claw of a beast," I mumbled to myself, while stepping closer to the horrific scene of slaughter.

I tried to control my breath and not panic. Blood was everywhere in the room. It seemed almost impossible that one person had contained so much blood. I forced myself to look at the face of the body. It was badly beaten, but I still recognized him from the photo. Now there was only one of them left. The question was, was he the next victim or the killer himself?

I looked away. I couldn't bear all that blood. And then I had a strange feeling. When did this murder happen?

Christian Junge-Larsen's eyes stared at the ceiling while I felt his wrist. There was no pulse, but he was warm.

The murder was not long ago.

I started looking around, feeling uneasy. Could the killer still be in the apartment? Was he looking at me, waiting to make his move? My breathing got heavier as I slowly, and without a sound, backed out of the room.

Then there was a noise and I turned around.

The back door.

I started running to the kitchen and found the back door. It was open and I heard something or somebody on the stairs. I should probably have stopped right there, I knew that. Everything inside me screamed STOP! But I didn't. I started running after the noise. What if it really was the killer? I couldn't miss the opportunity to see who he was.

So I ran.

With all the strength I could, I ran. I was in good shape, despite the extra pounds. I had always been in great shape and able to outrun most of my colleagues at the newspaper's annual sports event. I went quickly down the stairs and out another open door that led to the garbage cans. There were three big green ones in a corner in a closed courtyard. I stepped out. The yard was overgrown with weeds. The grass was brown and long dead. A tree in the middle had no leaves. A barbeque grill was old and rusty, forgotten by someone long ago. I looked carefully around me and saw only one way out through a big green gate.

It was still closed.

If the person on the stairs had opened it I would have heard it, but wasn't sure. I felt my heart pounding in my chest. Where the hell could he be?

Then another noise caught my attention. A glass of some sort hit the ground. It made an echo in the courtyard. I looked in the direction of the noise and was suddenly hit from behind by something big and heavy. After that, there was nothing but darkness and a sky of stars.

29

The headache wasn't the worst part about waking up. It was all the questions. The police had arrived in the meantime and found me on the floor of the apartment. How did I get there? I had no idea, I kept telling them.

"The killer must have carried me back up the stairs and put me here."

The police officer in front of me did not seem to believe any of what I was telling him.

"Why do you think I'm here, then?" I asked.

"All I know is that you are at a scene of crime and I need to know why."

Suddenly, I remembered I had checked the pulse and that my fingerprints would be on the body's wrist.

"I checked his pulse when I got here. You'd better know that."

"So you touched the body?"

"Yes, you will find my fingerprints on his wrist."

The officer looked at me with disbelief, and then he smiled.

"Are you okay?"

I touched the back of my head and got some blood on my fingers.

"It's nothing."

"Do you want us to take you to the hospital? You might need a couple of stitches," he said with a kinder voice.

"I'll be all right."

"Did you see anything that could be helpful to us? Did you see the face of the person who did this to you?"

I sighed and tried to rewind my memories. "I'm sorry. I am afraid he attacked me from behind."

"Why did you come here?"

"I wanted to do an interview with Christian Junge-Larsen."

The officer stared at me.

"Why?"

I sighed again. "It's a long story. Mostly because he went to school with Didrik Rosenfeldt, who was also killed a few days ago, just like two others were."

"So you think there's a connection between this murder and some other ones?" he asked with astonishment in his voice.

"I do, yes."

To my surprise, the officer immediately noted everything in his notebook. He seemed to actually take me seriously. That was a new one.

So I told him everything. All that I had found out on my own. I knew he wasn't an investigator; he was just first man on the scene and had to put everything in the report, but still it was the first time I felt like I'd met someone on the police force who was willing to listen.

Afterwards, the paramedics came and cleaned the back of my head. They kept saying they wanted me to come to the hospital for observation, that I might have sustained a slight concussion, but I refused. I had to get home to the kids and my dad, I said.

Just before I left, I saw the body being moved, and the officer from earlier came to talk to me.

"So I talked to my chief and he let me know that The National Police have taken over all four cases, and all four killings are now going to be investigated as one case."

I was impressed. "Did I have anything to do with that?"

"I suppose so," he answered.

"How?"

"I might be just an officer in a uniform, but I do have friends in higher places, and I told them what you told me."

I left the crime scene feeling dizzy because of the blow to my head, but also content that at least I had gotten somewhere with the police. Hopefully, it would in some way help Sune.

My daughter barely noticed I had come home when I entered the living room. She and Tobias had dressed up as a princess and a cowboy, Julie being the cowboy and Tobias being the princess. They were running around screaming and laughing. So I went into the kitchen where my dad sat reading the newspaper and listening to his favorite show on the radio. He looked so peaceful. He looked up when he heard me enter.

"Hi, sweetie. Do you want a cup?" he asked, and pointed at his own cup of coffee.

"I'm good," I said. "I'm just going to go upstairs and take a shower."

My dad stared at me with an investigative look.

"What?" I asked.

"Are you all right?"

"Sure."

He took a sip of his coffee.

"What happened to your head, then?"

I felt the back of my head. I had tried to wash away the blood at a sink in a restroom on the highway, but hadn't got rid of it all.

"A small accident, that's all."

"Are you sure it's nothing?"

"Really, it is nothing."

"Who did it?" Dad's voice started to sound concerned. I really didn't want him to worry about me. He recently had a stroke and his blood pressure was way too high. The last thing I wanted to do was to upset him.

"It was just an accident. Really."

I was the worst liar in the history of liars and my dad knew that. He put down the paper and stared at me over the top of his glasses.

"Are you in trouble?"

I shook my head, trying to be reassuring.

"No, no. Nothing like that at all. Just a little bump on the head, that's all."

"Did Peter have anything to do with it?"

"No, no. It wasn't Peter. I just hurt my head. That's all. I promise you have nothing to be worried about."

My dad sighed deeply.

"Is it that new guy you have been seeing? Did he do that to you?" Dad's voice was angry now.

I wanted to answer that it certainly wasn't, that he would never do such a thing. But I couldn't.

"He's a good guy, Dad. I'll be fine, really. I just need to take that shower."

"What's wrong, Mom?"

My daughter and Tobias had entered the kitchen from the other side. I closed my eyes.

"Someone hit her in the back of the head, and she doesn't want to tell us who it was," my dad said.

I looked at him. Was he kidding me? Why would he tell Julie? She would just be awake all night worrying about me.

"Listen up, everybody," I said with great authority. "I am a grown woman, capable of taking care of myself. I was just at the wrong place at the wrong time today, and someone, I don't know who it was, hit me with a rock on the back of my head. Nothing to worry about. It won't happen again."

My daughter looked at me with her big blue eyes.

"Why did you even go there alone? You always tell me not to go anywhere all alone."

"I know, sweetie, but I'm an adult, and I had to go there to do an interview. It was for my work."

They were all quiet. Then Tobias said something.

"When is my dad coming to get me?"

I squatted in front of him.

"Soon, sweetheart. Very soon."

"But Tobias gets to spend the night, right?" Julie asked.

"Yes, dear," I said and hugged them both. "How about we all go out for dinner tonight?"

Julie started jumping up and down.

"Yeah, let's get pizza!"

"But first, Mom has to go upstairs and get that shower."

30

The local Italian restaurant wasn't too shabby. Actually, it was very pleasant, and the atmosphere was charming in its way of trying to seem Italian but not really succeeding. I wondered about Giovanni. He wouldn't have liked this place. He once told me he didn't understand why people from Turkey or Iran who came to Denmark always started Italian restaurants when they weren't Italian at all and knew nothing about the Italian kitchen. He was right. I had been in Italy several times, and this food was not nearly as good.

But it was all right and my family and I had a good time. Luckily, no one asked any more questions. We just ate, drank, and laughed and talked about the kids' teachers in school, about a new project they were about to do, and about how they were mad at one tattle-tale boy in their class.

It was a nice evening and I enjoyed being with them. I thought about how much I loved my daughter and my dad. I enjoyed living with the two of them, and Tobias too, of course. I felt so sorry for him. He'd been missing his dad terribly as the days went by, and it was hard to explain why Sune didn't come to get him and take him home.

Since the place was close to my dad's home, we had walked there, and on the way home I held Julie's hand in mine. She looked at me with a happy smile and I saw such warmth and love in them that it filled me with happiness. This was it. It didn't get much better than this.

THE FEELING DIDN'T last long, though. Entering my dad's house, I knew immediately that something was terribly wrong. My first clue was that all the jackets from the closet in the hall were taken out and thrown on the floor at the entrance. Then there were the overturned chairs, the magazines on the floor, an overthrown lamp, and pillows and books all over the living room floor. A mirror had been broken and was in pieces.

"Wait here," I said to the others, while I inspected the rest of the house.

Everywhere, my dad's stuff had been thrown on the floor. The living room especially was a total mess. I almost started crying. To see my childhood home like this was hard. I knew my dad would be so upset. Here he had all the memories of his life with his wife and my mom—more than forty years of memories. I picked up a lamp from the floor and put it back on a table. Then I got a book from the floor. It was a photo album with pictures of my parents, my sister, and me from our trip to Marseille in France. They were ripped out and torn. I tried to pick up the pieces and found a part of a picture with my mom's face. A tear rolled down my cheek. Who would do such a thing?

"It's a bitch when someone messes with what you care about, right? When someone just rips away what you love and ruins your life."

The voice came from the chair in the corner. I knew it a little too well.

"Peter," I said.

He got up. "I told you not to leave me."

He took a couple of steps towards me. I dropped the photo album on the floor and backed up.

"What are you doing here?"

"Getting my family back."

"Why would you do this?" I pointed at the mess on the floor. I was furious. Who the hell did he think he was?

"The question is, why would you leave me? Why won't you obey me?"

"Are you kidding me? Is that how you're trying to win me back? 'Cause it really isn't working."

He took another step in my direction. This time I didn't back up. I didn't want to give him the pleasure of sensing my fear.

"I don't care," he hissed. "You are my wife, and you are going to come home with me, now."

"Aye, aye, captain. Is that what you want me to say? Is that what I am to you? A soldier? Property? What? Tell me?"

Peter sighed. The expression on his face changed suddenly. He was quiet for a second. His eyes were red. Had he been crying?

"Don't you get it?" he said with a quieter voice.

"No. I really don't think I do."

He sighed again. "Don't you get that I don't know what else to do? What to say to make you come back? You and Julie. I miss you. I can't stand being all alone in the house."

He came toward me with a sudden move and it made me jump back. Then he grabbed me and tried to kiss me. I pushed him away.

"Peter, for crying out loud."

He grabbed my hand and kissed it.

"Don't you know how much I love you? I've even been seeing a counselor who has been helping me. That is how much I love you. I've done it for you, Rebekka."

"Stop it!" I said and took back my hand. "You sent two of your hired soldiers to scare me and you trashed this house. Look at this place! Look at what you've done."

"I sent Johnny and Simon to try to get you to come back. I regret and am very sorry for that. But, this mess? I didn't do that," he said, much to my surprise. "It was like this when I got here. The front door was wide open."

"But you...you said...?"

I didn't get any further before we were interrupted.

"Oh, my God. What happened here?" Dad asked. He was confused, and I could tell he was upset. I turned a chair back upright and he sat in it, shaking his head at the mess.

"I don't understand. Who would do such a thing?"

I grabbed his hand. "I'll take care of it."

"Dad??" Julie's happy scream filled the room.

Peter turned and looked at her. "Sweetie pie!"

She ran toward him and grabbed his right leg.

"I've missed you so much," she said. "Did you come to scare away the bad guys who did this to Grandpa's house?"

Peter took her in his strong arms and lifted her up. Then he kissed her belly and she laughed.

"I sure did," he said. "I sure did."

Julie looked at me with big puppy eyes.

"Mommy, can Daddy stay? Please?"

I looked at him and sighed. I was still afraid of what he might be up to. He wasn't well and I couldn't trust him. But it was good for Julie to be with her dad again. That was important and I had to think of that as well.

"Please?" he said with the same voice as Julie.

I wasn't sure of my decision, but I took a chance. "Okay, then."

They both started cheering.

"But he's sleeping on the couch."

I DIDN'T GET much sleep that night. First, I had to clean up the mess, and that took several hours. Peter was nice enough to help me while Dad took the kids upstairs and put them to bed. When we were done cleaning and the house almost looked like itself again, I told Peter I wanted to go to bed, but he took out a bottle of my dad's wine and opened it.

"I'm not sure that's such a good idea," I said, knowing what normally happened to Peter when he had too much to drink.

"Just one glass?" he begged.

"Okay, just the one," I said.

We sat down in the kitchen and he poured two glasses.

"Cheers," he said.

"Cheers."

We drank and were quiet for a few seconds. I looked at him. He looked nice, but like he had gotten five years older in a short time. Maybe this had been harder on him than I thought. I was so mad about what he did to us that I never thought about his feelings. But how was I ever to trust him again?

"So how have you been?" I asked.

"Horrible."

"It hasn't been easy on us either."

He took my hand. "Listen. I know I've been an idiot. I know I need help. But I can't make it without you and Julie. You are my life. Without you two, there's nothing left to live for."

"You locked us in the basement, Peter. It is not very easy to trust you again."

He sighed and let go of my hand.

"I know. I'm sorry. I don't know what happened to me. Why I reacted that way. But I'm working on it, okay?"

"Okay."

We chatted and talked for hours, and for a while it felt just like old times. Almost, that is. I remembered what I used to love about him and I saw glimpses of that old Peter during the night. I told him all about Julie, her new school and new friends, and I could feel how much he had missed her. I started to feel badly for him. It wasn't fair to Julie either that I had robbed her of her own dad.

After three glasses of wine, I finally called it a night.

"Goodnight," he said, and walked to the kitchen sink, where he started washing up our wine glasses.

"It was really nice talking to you again," I said on my way out.

He looked at me from the sink. "I thought so too."

"Goodnight."

. . .

ALL NIGHT, I tossed and turned and thought. What if he really had changed? What if that counseling actually had helped him? I used to love the man more than life. Could he get back to being the same again? Could we have it all back? Our family? Our great life? I didn't know. I wasn't sure I wanted to take the chance in case it failed again. It would be too hard on Julie. But he was still her father and she loved him.

As did I.

31

When I got downstairs the next morning, my dad and Peter were sitting alone in the kitchen. Their conversation stopped when I walked in. They both looked at me and smiled.

"Don't stop on account of me," I said.

"It's okay," Peter said and got up. "I was just telling your dad I really appreciate his hospitality, and that I will no longer be a burden for you. I will be going back to Aarhus later today."

I was surprised. "Oh, okay," I said, and poured myself a cup of freshly made coffee and put a piece of toast on my plate.

He grabbed my shoulder. "I have some business to attend to, but if it is okay with you, I would like to come and visit again on the weekend. I'll get a room at the hotel this time." He let go of me. Then he stretched his back as if it was sore. "I'm too old for a couch anyway."

I smiled. It was strange, but I was happy that he was coming back. I hated to admit it, but I had missed him.

AT THE OFFICE, I got some very happy news. Sune had been released and was on his way back to the office. Just as I walked through the door, Sara told me with great excitement that his new lawyer had gotten him out. The lawyer apparently had heard that the National Police had taken over the case and they thought the four killings were related. Then she had argued that Sune was in jail when the last man was killed, and therefore couldn't be the murderer. The police had bought the argument and said he was still under suspicion, but a free man for now, as long as he didn't leave the country.

Sara had bought a big cinnamon cake at the nearby bakery and put a flag on Sune's desk and computer. She gave me a flag to hold in my hand and started waving hers as Sune entered the room.

"Surprise! Congratulations on getting out of jail," Sara yelled, while waving the flag. Then she hugged him.

He looked quite surprised, but also glad.

"Thank you, Sara. For everything," he said, and then he looked at me and gave me a hug. "And thank you too."

"You are very welcome," I said, as we sat down and Sara cut the cake.

"So how are you?"

"I can't wait to see Tobias when he is done with school today. Has he been behaving well?"

"He's the best. Julie is going to cry her heart out when she learns that he is not going to sleep in her room any longer. So is my dad, I think."

Sune laughed.

"He'll be back another time."

"I know he will."

"So, how did they treat you in the slammer?" Sara asked.

I ate my piece of the cake. A little too heavy on the cinnamon, if you ask me, but otherwise it was okay.

Sune laughed. "They treated me all right, I guess."

"Did they beat you?"

He laughed again. "No, they did not. It's not like the movies. They were strict and questioned me a lot, which was unpleasant. I answered them I realized I sounded more and more like I could actually have done it. I've wanted to kill him for years. I wanted to do exactly what was done to him."

"Did you tell them that?" Sara asked with her mouth full.

"I did. I was honest and that almost got me into a lot of trouble. But luckily I had a good lawyer who kept her ears and eyes open."

"That was great," I said. "So, you're all right now?"

"Yes, ma'am."

"I'm glad to hear that, because I have a lot to tell you. We have a killer to catch so we can prove your innocence."

I told Sune everything that had happened since he was locked up —the dead body I walked in on in Elsinore, the man I tried to follow down the stairs, and the attack from behind that left me unconscious.

"You shouldn't have gone there alone," Sune said.

"No, so I've heard." I got up and got my purse. I found the photo of the boarding school boys. I showed it to Sune.

"Only one is left now," I said.

He nodded. "I know. Do you think he's the killer?"

"I don't know. He didn't strike me as the type. But, then again, who does?"

"You're right. He doesn't fit the profile of someone who would weld his own cross of spikes. But maybe he could have had someone else do it."

"That's a possibility."

"What about Irene?"

"She has a pretty good motive. But is she strong enough to carry me up the stairs? She's not a big woman."

"Maybe she had help."

"Mmm...I don't know. I didn't get the sense there was more than one person in the apartment when I was there. But I did tell the police about my suspicion toward her and Ulrik Gyldenlove, and I just hope they will talk to them."

"You could talk to both of them again."

"I know. Maybe I should. But the killer knows me now and knows I am on to him. He's probably the one who messed up my father's house. I don't know who else it would be. But that means I have to be careful. I have a family to think of. I think it was a warning."

Sune nodded pensively. "It might have been. You really have to be careful now."

I thought about the fact that if it was the killer who had messed up my dad's house, then it meant he knew where I lived. That made me scared for my daughter and father.

"So, what do you suggest that we do?"

"Well, I've been doing a lot of thinking in jail and I didn't come up with much. But I have one idea. It might not lead to anything, but it's worth a try."

I looked at him and finished my coffee. "Yes?"

"It's a small thing and might not help us in any way. But I thought about looking into the pastor's computer."

I smiled. "Looking into? As in hacking yourself into?"

"You know what I mean," he said. "Maybe we'll find something that could give us a clue."

"You know, if the police find out they could lock you up again," Sara said with a concerned voice.

Sune nodded. "I know that very well. But I have to do something. The police still have me on their list of suspects. They even argued that I might have had an accomplice on the outside to commit the last murder. They haven't let me off the hook just yet, and I might be arrested again if there's another killing now. I don't have anything to lose anymore, as far as I can see."

I totally understood what he was saying. He'd been sitting in the jail for days without being able to do anything. Now he wanted to clear his name. He'd been wrongfully imprisoned once before and that had almost ruined his life. This time he would fight to the end.

32

What Sune found on the prison pastor's computer wasn't a pretty sight. It only took him two hours to hack into it. He showed me some of what he found. Most of it was short movies of real killings and torture. Sometimes it was men, sometimes women, and even sometimes small children, all taped somewhere far away by someone who was willing to kill and torture for money. They were all bad quality, like they were recorded on a cell phone or a really old camera.

"This is horrifying," I said, as Sune played me one of the videos. It showed a group of young boys beating up a homeless man until he didn't move anymore. One of them recorded everything on a cell phone.

"I know," he answered. "But that stuff turns some people on for some weird reason we will probably never understand. And they are willing to pay a lot of money for it."

"This turns them on?"

"Yes. The screams of pain are arousing to them."

"You mean they get off on someone being tortured and killed?"

"I'm afraid so."

I leaned back in my chair with a strange feeling in my stomach.

How could anyone be so sick?

"You're right. I'll never understand that. It's too disgusting."

I LEFT Sune at the computer and went to the kitchen to get some water. Then I sat at my own desk and tried to get my thoughts straight. Giovanni had tried to call me again a couple of times and Sara had left four notes telling me to call him back before she went insane. Maybe it was true what they said. The more you played hard to get, the more he wanted you.

So I decided to call him back.

"Finally," he said with that cute accent of his. "Where have you been? I've called and called."

"I know. I've been very busy."

"I know you have a busy job, but I get so worried about you."

I had to admit I didn't think he would actually worry about me.

"So when can I see you?" he asked.

I looked at the picture of the welded cross Sune had printed for me. It was lying on the desk in front of me. My stomach acted up again. What if it really was Giovanni in the apartment? What if he hit me in the courtyard and carried me back to the apartment to make me look suspicious? What if he only wanted to see me now so he could finish me off?

"It's better that we lay low for a couple of days," I said.

"What are you saying?"

I almost felt his disappointment through the phone. "I just mean that it might be better to take a little break from each other. My ex-husband is coming this weekend, and I don't want to confuse Julie too much."

"Your ex-husband? What does that mean? Are you getting back together with him?"

"I don't know right now. I just know that everything is a little complicated and I need time to think."

"So that's it? Just like that?"

"I don't know yet."

"But you must have some feelings for him, since you're telling me to stay away from you. Something I find impossible to do."

I sighed and rubbed my forehead. A headache was beginning to take shape.

"Just give me a week, all right? That's all I am asking."

"Okay. Don't take too long, though."

"I won't. I promise."

I HUNG UP FEELING LOUSY. I had no idea what was going on with me and I hated that. I was used to being in control of my emotions. I didn't like this situation.

"Everything A-Okay?" Sune asked without looking up from his computer. His fingers danced on the keyboard.

"I'm fine." I sighed.

"You don't sound fine."

"It's nothing."

"I might have something that might cheer you up."

I looked at him with anticipation. "Really?"

"Really."

I went to his desk. "So, what is it?"

Sune clicked the mouse and a list of names showed on the screen.

"What am I looking at? I don't get it."

"Look at the names."

I read them out loud.

"Zenia Damsgaard, Zenia Larsen, Zenia Emborg, Zenia Busck, Zenia Peterson." I stopped. "It just goes on like that, the same first name, different last names."

"These are names he has been searching for on the internet...on Google and the yellow pages. So what does that tell us?"

"That he's looking for someone named Zenia?"

"Very good. Yes, that's exactly what he has been doing. From his internet history, I can tell that he has been searching a lot for Zenia and found nine girls with that name in Denmark. I have gathered all of them."

"So?"

"So why would he search for a girl for whom he only knows the first name?"

"Because he met her in a bar maybe and she only gave him her first name. Since it's a relatively rare name, he thought he could find her on the internet. Maybe he was in love. Who knows?"

"That's one theory. But what about this? Maybe it's because he used to know her when she was younger and still in school, and now he figures she has gotten married, and therefore changed her last name."

I nodded. It sounded like a possibility. But I didn't quite see how it helped us.

"I know what you're thinking," Sune said. "But I just feel like it might have something to do with our case."

"Look," I said and pointed at one of the names.

"Zenia Clausen," Sune read out loud.

Our eyes met.

"Clausen?"

"Could that be...?" Sune looked back at the screen.

"Like in Bjorn Clausen?" I said.

"A sister?"

"He didn't have a sister as far as I know," I said. "Maybe it could have been a cousin? Can you find her on the yellow pages and maybe get a name or a number?"

Sune typed, then leaned back and touched his Mohawk with the tip of his fingers.

"Nothing."

I thought for a second.

"Try to look her up in Folkeregistret, where the Danish government keeps everybody registered."

"Great idea," Sune said and leaned forward. Now he was typing again with great eagerness.

I went to have a cigarette at the window in the kitchen. I thought about my sister as I looked out at the people in the street in their long coats. If Bjorn had a sister, she probably knew her. She knew all girls her own age from this town back then. So I called my sister, but she didn't answer the phone. I left her a message and killed my cigarette.

When I went back to Sune, I brought two cups of fresh coffee.

"Here you go," I said, when I put it on the desk in front of him. He didn't notice it. He stared at the screen.

"You better see this," he said.

I went behind his back and looked at the screen. He pointed at a date.

"Zenia Clausen died twenty years ago. In April 1991."

MY HEAD WAS SPINNING. Was it another death related to the five others? Was she killed? In the register, it said Zenia Clausen had committed suicide in 1991. It said she had a child in 1987. A baby boy. In '87 she would have been only 17. The father was unknown.

The last important thing I got out of the register was that she wasn't born Clausen. Before her marriage to a Michael Clausen in 1987, her last name was Petersen. So she wasn't a sister or a cousin. I remembered Sune's conversation with the boarding school headmaster. Bjorn Clausen had a brother who went to the school as well. Michael Clausen. It must have been him. She married Bjorn's brother.

So what did it all mean?

The pastor was looking for her, but why? Didn't he know she was dead? Maybe he didn't. Maybe he didn't even know she had married Michael.

"Pastor Bertel Due-Lauritzen was gay," Sune said suddenly.

I looked at him with surprise.

"What?"

"Everybody knew he was gay," he said. "He tried to hide it, but we all knew."

"How did you know?"

"You can't hide a thing like that in a prison filled with young boys."

"I see. So he didn't search for Zenia because she was his old school flame? It was something else that made him look for her."

Sune nodded. "It must have been."

33

We had a late lunch at the restaurant at the port. I was so happy to have Sune back, I wanted to treat him and Sara to a nice lunch. I had cleared it with my editor. The newspaper would pay.

We each had a stjerneskud, fish on rye bread with shrimp and remoulade on top. It was very good. We all enjoyed a beer with it. It was too cold to sit outside, but we enjoyed the view of the old fishing boats from inside. An old fisherman with orange overalls worked on his boat. I remembered how I used to love coming down here as a child and watching the different people. There were fishermen on the old boats, rich people on the yachts, and drunkards sitting on a bench drinking beer all day. People fished from the pier, nicely dressed ladies walked their dogs with big hats, and joggers ran by. A port always attracted a lot of life, especially in the summer when all the tourists and rich people came from up north. Just a few months from now, the place would be crawling with them again.

I had grown to like the quiet. I was glad I had come back. The big city wasn't for me anymore. And maybe, just maybe, it wasn't for Peter anymore either. Maybe I could get him to move down here if we were to become a family again. I would like that. I had given it a lot of thought. If he was willing to change and we could go to a counselor, I might be willing to consider getting back with him. Maybe.

In the middle of lunch, my phone rang. It was my dad. I got up and took it.

"Is something wrong with Julie?"

He was breathing heavily in the phone. Something was definitely wrong. It wasn't good for his heart to get agitated.

"She wasn't there when I went to pick her up from school."

My heart was pounding so I almost couldn't breathe.

"What...why...where is she then?"

"The school said she had already been picked up."

"Picked up?" My head started to spin. "By whom?"

I could hear my dad trying to catch his breath.

"Her dad."

SUNE LOOKED at me when I got back to the table. "What's wrong?"

I sat down. I felt like the whole restaurant was spinning around me.

"It's Julie."

I looked for Peter's number under my contacts in my cell phone.

"What happened?" Sara asked.

"Peter took her from school."

"Who is Peter?" Sara asked.

"The ex," Sune whispered to her.

I found Peter and tried to call. No one answered. Just as I expected.

"That son of a..." Sune said with an angry voice.

"I'm going to kill him," I said, while trying to call him again. Still, no answer. Just the machine. I left an angry message and hung up.

"How could he pick her up from school if the teachers didn't know him?" Sara asked. "They have never seen him before."

"They told my dad he came to her classroom. When she saw him, she got all exited and yelled out 'Dad,' so they had no second thoughts about letting her go with him."

"They should still have called you," Sune said. "Did you call the police?"

"My dad did, but there's not much they can do right now."

"Well, maybe he just missed her and took her somewhere nice," Sara said. "Like to get ice cream."

My heart still pounded and the thoughts lined up in my head. Why would he do this to me now? If he wanted to win me back, this was the stupidest thing he could do. So maybe Sara was right. Maybe he just wanted to spend time with her. But why didn't he call me first? He's not that stupid and he would know I would worry. No, I knew Peter. This was either a warning or he had actually taken her. That was the scary part. Where would he take her? He wouldn't be so stupid as to take her with him back to Aarhus, would he?

I called him again. Still just a machine. I left another message, trying to tone myself down a little and talk nicely.

"Julie is missing, Peter. If you have her, please call me and let me know that she is all right," I heard myself say in a gentle voice, as gently as I could, given the circumstances, that is.

A second later, a text came on my phone: I have her. She's fine. She will stay with me from now on. She's my daughter too.

I felt like all the blood disappeared from my face. What the hell was he thinking? If he wanted custody of Julie, why didn't he just hire a lawyer and drag me through the system? What had happened to the man I used to love? Had he totally lost it?

The two others noticed my pale face.

"Now what?" Sune asked and grabbed my hand.

I showed them the text. Sune got an angry expression on his face.

I felt so anxious. I knew he wouldn't harm her, but would I ever see her again?

"Would you help me find her?" I asked, and Sune nodded without hesitation.

I WENT to the local police station and talked to my friend there. Detective Michael Oestergaard greeted us and we sat down in his small office. On his desk, he had a picture of a beautiful woman and a boy a little younger than Julie. Probably his wife and kid, I thought, and almost started crying, thinking about what had happened to my family during the last year.

Detective Oestergaard was very nice and sympathetic and all, but he couldn't do much, he said.

"Your ex-husband will probably bring her back within the next twenty-four hours. That's how these cases normally go."

"Maybe with a normal husband," I said.

"Listen, Rebekka." The detective leaned back in his chair with an annoyingly arrogant smile I hadn't noticed before. Maybe it was just because of the situation and the pressure, but suddenly I didn't like him so much anymore. He seemed a little creepy.

"On paper, you and Peter are still married, so he is entitled to pick your daughter up from school, as long as he doesn't hurt her. It's a fight between two people in a marriage. As a police officer, I have no right to interfere. That's just the way it is."

"But he is not allowed to keep her from me, right?"

"That's right. But you have to fight him through the system. Take him to court. The police can't do much, as I already said. Unless you think he is harming her in any way, of course."

I got up from the chair feeling helpless.

"I'm sorry," Michael Oestergaard said, as Sune shook his hand.

So was I. I knew I had to get her back on my own.

34

S une had to drive. I was too upset. My hands were shaking and my heart wouldn't stop pounding. I was scared. Where was she? I had only one place to look for her—our old house in Aarhus where Peter now lived alone. The same house I had run from not long ago, the same house where my husband had locked us in the basement.

"Why didn't you just get a divorce?" Sune asked.

"I don't know." I sighed. "I didn't think he would give me one. I just wanted to get away in a hurry and deal with everything later. Maybe I hoped that he wouldn't find us. That he wouldn't look for us."

Sune looked at me and smiled.

"I know. I was stupid."

"I know how you felt. You just had to get away, right? Start all over."

I smiled a little. He was exactly right. If anyone understood, it was Sune.

IT WAS dark when we drove into Aarhus, the city of smiles, as it was called. There was not much to smile about right now. We hit the beach line and neared my old house on L.P. Bechsvej. It was close to the ocean, but not oceanfront, as I had always wanted. We paid more for it than many of the oceanfront houses, but Peter wanted this one. It was old and big. A white house with a black glazed-tile roof. It was beautiful and even majestic, but it wasn't me.

I felt a chill up my back as we drove over the gravel in the driveway. This had once been my personal prison. Was Julie in there now? Was he keeping her in that same basement?

I ran out of the car and rang the doorbell. Then I got impatient and knocked frantically on the thick old black wooden door. I really longed to hold my daughter in my arms.

"Peter!" I yelled. "Open up!"

It took awhile for the door to open. Peter stood in the doorway. He smiled a weird manic smile and I froze. He wasn't well. That I was sure of. The Peter I had seen the day before in my dad's living room was gone again. Or had this crazy Peter been there all the time? Had he just been manipulating me into thinking he was doing better?

"Where is she?" I asked, and pushed him aside as I ran into the hall. "What have you done to her?"

Peter turned around and kept smiling at me.

"Where is she?" I yelled.

Then he hushed me. "Shh. She's sleeping."

"What? It's seven-thirty. Why would she be asleep?" I stopped and looked at him.

"Unless you sedated her? Did you do that, Peter? Did you?"

He didn't say anything. He didn't have to.

"Peter!"

"She was crying so loud in the car when I told her we were going back to our old house, and she said she wanted her mother, and yada, yada, yada. So, yes, I slipped her a sleeping pill in her soda on the way."

His eyes and hands could not hold still. I backed up a bit. Sune stood in the doorway.

"You're high on something." I studied his large pupils.

"So what? Little miss high-and-mighty?"

"So, I don't want you to be near my daughter like this, not ever!" I yelled. "I can't believe I almost trusted you again. I was even willing to give you a second chance. And now you do this?"

"So, why did you?"

"Because maybe I saw something in you, maybe I saw that Peter I used to know, that sweet husband and amazing father, who I used to love."

I RAN UP THE STAIRS. When I reached the bedroom, I opened the door and was at once relieved. In her old bedroom, Julie was asleep in her childhood bed. My heart stopped pounding for the first time in many hours. There she was. Safe and sound asleep.

I went to her and put my ear to her chest. I wanted to hear her little heart, and feel that she was alive and well. But, as I did, I knew right away that something was very wrong. It was beating too slowly. I checked her pulse on her neck. It was weak. Had Peter given her a sleeping pill for adults? I knew he used to take pills like that when he had problems sleeping. But they were way too strong. That was too much for such a small body.

I was scared and took her in my arms to carry her out of the room.

Then I heard turmoil in the hall, and when I got to the stairs, I saw Peter and Sune fighting on the marble floor.

"Are you kidding me?" I yelled. "Call for an ambulance immediately!"

Both of them stopped and got up from the floor.

"What's wrong?" Peter asked.

I walked down the stairs carefully with Julie in my arms. I heard Sune calling for an ambulance. His voice sounded desperate and that made me even more scared.

"You gave her too much," I said, almost crying, but trying to hold it back. I had to keep my head clear and not let my emotions run away with me.

I saw Peter's expression change at once. He was scared now too.

I gently put Julie down on the floor, while talking to her and caressing her head...trying to wake her up.

"Please don't die on me," I cried. "Please, God, save her."

35

It seemed like it took forever to pump my baby's stomach. Peter sat with us in the waiting room at the ER at Skejby Hospital. He hid his face in his hands.

"I just wanted to spend a little time with her," he kept mumbling. His hands kept dancing around his face and hair. He definitely wasn't well, I thought. Maybe this could be a wake-up call for him. Maybe now he would realize he needed help. Whatever happened to him during his time in Iraq, he had to do something about it now.

Either that or he would lose everything. I had recently read in a newspaper that several men, all former soldiers, were now living in the forest in Denmark. They didn't want to be a part of society any longer. They didn't know how. A lot of others became criminals and drug addicts because they missed the excitement, the thrill of being in a war zone. The adrenaline was like a drug for them. And they had a hard time functioning without it.

And they were too proud to ask for help. Soldiers fight and kill. They're not supposed to be running back home having problems. They are heroes.

Peter was just like that.

"Rebekka Franck?" The voice belonged to a doctor in a white coat. She was tall and serious looking.

I got up from my chair. "Yes?"

The doctor cleared her throat. "Your daughter is stable now, but we have to keep her for observation."

The weight of the world fell off my shoulders.

"Oh, my God. Thank you," I said.

The doctor kept her serious look. It made me scared. Julie's condition was life-threatening, she said.

"We pumped a lot of Demerol out of her stomach. It is a strong sleeping drug that is known to have serious side effects. I must say, it's very dangerous to give to a little child as small as Julie."

"What kind of side effects?"

"They are very addictive, and if used for a longer period of time, they can cause psychosis, a strong mental disorder."

I looked at Peter. He'd been taking these pills as long as I could remember. With both the pills and his mental problems from the war, it was a dangerous cocktail. I began to understand his condition.

"So, what about Julie? Has it caused her any damage?"

"I don't think so."

Once again, I felt relieved, but worried.

"Will she have any withdrawal symptoms from having the drug, even though it was only this one time?"

The doctor nodded and that made my heart jump.

"Probably a little bit for a day or two. But then she will be fine. She might be a little cranky and have trouble sleeping, but after a couple of days, she will be back to her old self."

"I'm glad to hear that."

"But I have to say that I have contacted Social Services and told them about Julie's condition. They will be in touch with you soon. It's very serious to drug your kids."

I looked at Peter again. I could tell he was listening to the conversation. He had started crying. I saw no need for me to tell that it was him. In some ways, I had a responsibility for this too. I had seen him take these pills for years and not stopped him. How could I have been so blind?

"I know," I said. "It won't happen again."

"I sure hope it won't." The doctor disappeared down the hall again.

JULIE LOOKED SO small and weak when I went into her room a few hours later. She was pale and exhausted.

"Can we go home now?" she asked with the tiny voice she always had whenever she was sick.

"Soon, sweetheart." I kissed her forehead and looked into her bright blue eyes.

"Daddy didn't mean to drug me. It was an accident, Mom," she said.

I kissed her again. "Of course it was."

"So I get to see him again, right?"

"Of course. He's waiting outside. He wants to say hello to you."

She smiled and showed where her two front teeth had fallen out.

"Is it okay with you, Mom?"

"Of course it is. But be gentle with him. He's very sad about what happened." I kissed her again and went outside.

"She's all yours," I said to Peter.

He got up from the chair. Then he stopped and took a step backwards. I saw it in his expression, but couldn't believe it. Couldn't believe what he was about to do.

"Peter?"

"I'm sorry."

He held his coat between his hands and took another step away from me.

"Peter, damn it. She is waiting for you!" I pleaded and begged him not to do this, but he had already made up his mind. He was going to abandon us.

"I can't face her," he said, backing up even more.

I felt desperate. There had to be something I could do to stop him from breaking Julie's fragile heart.

"Peter, you can't just leave her. At least say goodbye before you go."

"Tell her I'm sorry."

I felt like I would explode. Who the hell did a thing like that? I wanted to scream at him, yell that he was being so selfish and his daughter would cry her heart out after this. I wanted to beat some sense into him, tell him Julie had already forgiven him, and tell him that as long as he got professional help, everyone would forgive him. If that didn't work, I wanted to ask him if this was really the way he wanted Julie to remember him, as the dad who took her without my knowledge, and then sedated her so she almost died. That was all she would remember of him. That and the fact that he later abandoned her while she was waiting for him in the hospital bed he put her in. I wanted her to know the dad I used to know. Because he was awesome. And it wasn't too late if he really wanted to. He could change.

Those were the things I was thinking about. Those were the things I wanted to have said. But I never did. Peter was already on his way. He just shook his head, then turned around and walked away.

Gone. Out of our lives. Out of Julie's life. As I watched his back disappear down the hall, I wondered if we would ever see him again.

36

A couple of days later, I finally got to take my baby with me back home to my dad's house in Karrebaeksminde. She had gotten the color back in her cheeks and smiled widely when she saw my dad standing outside his house. She almost jumped out of the car while it was still moving and jumped into his arms.

I was glad to see her smiling again. She had cried a lot when I told her that her dad was very sorry, but he wouldn't come and see her in the hospital.

"Will he come another day, then? Will he come and visit me at Grandpa's again?"

"I don't know, sweetheart."

I never was much of a liar and had a hard time keeping the truth from her...that he had left and I wasn't sure we would see him again.

I wasn't sure I even understood why Peter had reacted the way he had, so how could I explain it to her? Should I say that it was guilt? That he couldn't face her because he was so afraid because it was his fault that she almost died? That he was embarrassed? That he was a soldier and they don't make mistakes, they don't endanger other people's lives? They protect people. He was supposed to be able to protect his own family. And he failed.

I couldn't explain that to a six-year-old. But I sensed she somehow understood anyway.

"Did you tell him I'm not mad at him for giving me those pills?"

"Yes, I did, and he was very happy to hear that. But he just needed to take a little time to think about what happened. He told me to tell you that he loves you very much."

My heart had almost broken. She had forgiven him. But he couldn't forgive himself. Of all of us, she was the adult one.

SUNE AND TOBIAS came over later that same day. Tobias had made a whole bunch of drawings for Julie and brought her a box of chocolates. The kids ran screaming upstairs and I sat down in the kitchen with Sune and opened the chocolates. Julie wasn't much of a chocolate eater, but I was.

"So, how are you?" Sune asked.

"Heartbroken. But otherwise just hanging in there. And you?"

He smiled. "Loving every day of my freedom."

"Any news about your case?"

"Nope. My lawyer called me yesterday and said the police had another suspect now, but they didn't have anything concrete on this guy yet."

"How does she get all that information?"

"She told me she has a contact in the National Police."

"I see. Did you get a name?"

"Of the suspect or the contact?"

"The suspect, naturally."

"No, but I have a way of finding it out if you want me to."

I smiled and took another piece of chocolate. "Of course you do."

I poured myself a glass of red wine while Sune had a beer. We were pensive for a couple of minutes, while enjoying the noise of two happy kids playing together upstairs.

"So...do you want me to find that name for you right now?" He had read my mind. I was so curious.

"Yes! Let's do it now," I said, and cleared the table of stuff like my dad's word puzzles, old radio, and letters. All except my wine and Sune's beer.

Meanwhile, Sune got his laptop from his car.

The old cat stared at us over her bowl of food, while we hacked into the National Police server one more time. Sune had gotten good at this, I thought. But that was when it got dangerous. When hackers thought they had done it so many times it was a piece of cake, then they got sloppy and left a trace. Sune told me that in the beginning. Now I told him to remember it.

"I know, I know," he muttered.

I drank a sip of my wine and waited. Even when I tried to focus, I didn't get what it was he did on that computer. I could never do it. He was a magician, I thought.

And a pretty good one. A few minutes later, he had the name.

"Ulrik Gyldenlove," I read out loud.

"I knew it," Sune said.

"You and me both," I said, and wondered what they could have on him that made him a suspect.

"What does it say about him? Why is he a suspect?"

Sune clicked the mouse and read, "He used to be friends with all four of the deceased. He went to the same boarding school and he was the last living one from a gang of rich boys from the school who used to hang out together, and were accused of raping a local girl in 1985."

"All things we already know." I leaned back in the chair. Didn't they have anything besides what we had already figured out?

"IT ALSO SAYS they got all this information from the rape victim, Irene Hansen," Sune continued.

"So they talked to her, just like we did, and now they know about the gang and the game they played."

"A Gentleman Hunt?"

"Yes. But they must have something else on the guy. Look some more."

Sune's eyes returned to the screen. "They brought him in for questioning."

"Okay. What did that give them?"

Sune read again. "It seems as though he was open and honest with them. Just like he was with us. He told them everything in detail about what the group did and to whom. It's not pretty."

"They must have broken him during the interrogation," I said, as I got up from the chair. I felt like we were close to the answer right now. Ulrik Gyldenlove had killed the rest of the gang. Why? Because they each witnessed something that would harm him if it got out in public? No, then he would have done it long before. And he wouldn't tell the police all these details. Then what? What was it? I could only come up with one motive. It had to be revenge. I looked at Sune.

"What was it Gyldenlove said to me? Do you remember? I told you about it in the car on our way back," I said to him.

He looked up.

"Which part?"

"The part when I asked him if the gang had ever picked on him?"

"Oh, yeah. Something like you only pick on someone who won't fight back. Is that it?"

"That is exactly it. He is fighting back for something. Something they did to him back then."

"Like what?"

I shook my head. I didn't know. But it must have been something really bad. Enough for him to plan this type of revenge over the years and then execute his old friends one by one.

"So you think that Bjorn Clausen was the first one and then he waited twenty-four years to kill the next?"

"Something like that."

I stared at Sune with great excitement. We were almost there. I felt it.

"Maybe it's the rape. I mean, they were all in that picture from that night. Maybe he and Irene are in on it together."

Sune nodded.

"But why would she tell the police that he was there? Why would she tell us?"

Sune was right. Some things didn't add up yet. I sat down when my phone vibrated on the kitchen table. It was my sister returning my phone call from the other day.

"I'm so sorry for not calling you before, but I knew from Dad that Julie was in the hospital, so I thought it was better to wait."

My sister, the perfectionist. Always thinking of others. That's just how she was.

"So how is Julie?"

"Better. She's playing upstairs with her friend."

"I'm glad to hear that. I wanted to call you while you were up there, but Dad said you had shut off the phone to better concentrate on being there for Julie."

"That's right. Don't worry about it."

My sister and I had never been close. There were ten years between us and we'd never had an intimate relationship, so I would never have expected her to call me in the hospital anyway. But I was glad she said it.

"So you wanted to know something about Zenia?"

"Yes, do you know her?"

"I've heard about her."

"Great! Anything you remember would be a help."

I looked at Sune, who was intently reading his computer.

"She was a girl at the boarding school. Her parents were rich like most of the kids. They lived in London, so they put her in that school, which is the story of a lot of the kids there."

"I've heard about that."

"Anyway, it was a mess that ended in tragedy, as far as I know. She was a couple of years younger than Didrik Rosenfeldt and the gang; I heard that Ulrik Gyldenlove, who was one of the boys in the gang, had quite a crush on her. But she was in love with Bjorn Clausen's younger brother, Michael, who also went to the school."

"Whom she later married," I said.

169

"Yes...against her parents' protests. He wasn't good enough for her, in their eyes."

"Because he wasn't rich. He was there on a scholarship."

"Exactly."

"So she rejected Ulrik Gyldenlove?"

"Yes. Well not at first. The story goes that she played them both. Then she became pregnant at seventeen, but no one knew who the father was. It was a big scandal at the school, and she was expelled. Her parents disowned her. The only one who took care of her was Michael Clausen. He married her when they both turned eighteen, not knowing if the child was his."

"Wow. And I bet Ulrik Gyldenlove wouldn't have done that."

"No. His parents would have cut him off if he did that. He tried to pay her off. To get her to have an abortion, but she refused. He would have lost everything if he had married her. His inheritance, his status, his future, everything. He didn't dare risk that."

"But Michael Clausen had nothing to lose."

"No. But he was expelled from the school too because they were sure that he was the one who got her pregnant, since he was the one who married her."

"So he did lose something?"

"Yes. But he loved her like crazy."

"Then what happened?"

"She killed herself...and the child."

"Wow. That's tough."

"I know."

"What happened to Michael Clausen?

"Beats me. I haven't heard about him in ages."

I thanked my sister and hung up, promising to keep in touch and see each other soon, like we always promised, but never followed through.

I looked at Sune, who hadn't touched his beer since I picked up the phone.

"Zenia killed herself and her kid," I said. "She didn't know who the father was. It was either Michael Clausen, whom she married, or Ulrik Gyldenlove. Apparently she loved them both."

Sune looked up. "That's not how I would put it."

"What do you mean?" I took a sip of my red wine and almost choked on it when he answered me.

"It says here that Ulrik Gyldenlove admitted raping her."

I got up and went to look at the police report from the interrogation of Ulrik Gyldenlove. In it, he stated that he and the other boys raped a lot of girls. One of them was Zenia Petersen, who later became Zenia Clausen.

My head started spinning. Not because of the wine, but the thoughts made me dizzy. Had Ulrik Gyldenlove killed Zenia and her child to make sure no one ever knew what he had done? Perhaps he didn't want the boy seeking him out later claiming he was his dad. Was money a motive? And then did he kill his friends because they knew as well? Because they would blackmail him? If that was true, he knew if his family found out he would lose everything. But most of the boys in the gang had their own money. Like Didrik Rosenfeldt. He didn't need to blackmail anyone. Maybe he killed them because they raped her too. Maybe he wanted vengeance because he loved her. Was that the reason?

And where was Michael Clausen? Could Gyldenlove have killed him too out of jealousy but the body was never found?

I was tired and sat down in the chair. I ate a piece of chocolate and drank the rest of my wine.

Ulrik Gyldenlove was still a free man. If he was the killer, who would be his next victim?

37

Ulrik Gyldenlove was not a happy man. He never had been and probably never would be. Not even when he married his beautiful aristocratic wife, Sacha, much to his parent's satisfaction. Not even when his daughter Caroline was born and he got to hold her in his arms for the first time. He just wasn't cut out to be a happy man.

For that, he carried too much baggage.

And over the last couple of weeks, seeing his old friends die one after another didn't seem to make him any happier. He had thought it would, though. He had always thought they deserved exactly what they were getting now.

Why would he want them to die? Because they made him do it. They pushed him. He never wanted to rape Zenia. He loved her. But Didrik—that bastard—thought she needed to be punished for rejecting Ulrik. And Ulrik had enjoyed the idea of having her suffer a little bit for all the heartbreak she had caused him, for refusing to love him even though he had tried everything. He tried buying her things. He would take her out to nice places for dinner. He even bought her a ring, but she didn't want it. She didn't love him the way he loved her. For that, he, in a way, wanted what happened to her.

But he could never have imagined what would happen next.

Ever since that night at the boarding school gym when he raped her on the floor while the others held her down, he had a sadness inside—one that never would go away.

And it grew in him when he heard Zenia was pregnant. It grew even bigger when he tried to pay her off to get an abortion. Another one of Didrik Rosenfeldt's bright ideas.

But the worst part was when she married that boy, Michael Clausen. Not that Ulrik could have married her himself. That never would have been even considered. It simply was not an option. But that she would choose him, that little good-for-nothing boy who had no money. Ulrik would never understand.

And it broke his heart.

Now they were all gone. Bjorn Clausen, Didrik Rosenfeldt, Henrik Holch, Bertel Due-Lauritzen, Christian Junge-Larsen, and even Zenia Petersen. He would have thought that would have given him some peace of mind. That it would maybe even give him some sort of happiness to see them go.

But it didn't.

He was still sad. He'd been like that for years now...twenty-five years, to be exact. And it didn't seem like it was about to change for him. It was as if his life only got worse as the years went by. He had suffered trying to escape his past for too long now. It was time to face the music. Especially now, since his wife had died a couple of years ago. Now only he and his daughter, Caroline, were left. She would go to London next year to business school.

Then he would be all alone.

Alone with his own miserable self. The person he loathed most in this world. The only one he could never escape.

Was it worth it? Was anything he had done in his life worth it? No. None of it had been. But that was life, right? A series of events that happened to you while you were busy making plans for your future. And then life came along and all the dreams were gone. Crushed into pieces. Eventually they would be forgotten, and people learned that life was all about getting by. Coping. Surviving.

Nothing else.

It was called growing up, his father had said.

Ulrik was thinking about all that when he got himself ready for the evening. It was going to be an important night. Maybe the most important one in his miserable little life. Then he picked up the phone.

It was finally time to finish it all off.

38

Sune and Tobias stayed for dinner. Julie convinced Sune that Tobias just had to have another sleepover. She needed him in order to get really well, she said. Fortunately for her, he agreed.

My dad made a traditional Danish dish called frikadeller, meatballs with potatoes and a brown gravy. It was horrible. My dad had never been the best cook, and even though I helped him make it, he put too much salt in it, which made it almost inedible. But no one said anything during dinner, and I appreciated that. I didn't like to see my dad's feelings get hurt.

So when he asked if we liked it, everybody—even the kids—said it was delicious. And Dad was very happy when he went upstairs to go to bed.

Sune and I laughed and I drank some more red wine while Sune had a Coke. Then we tucked the kids in and turned on the TV.

I liked Sune's company. And he seemed to like mine. We were ten years apart in age and very far apart in personality, but we still enjoyed being near one another. He was so easy to be with. Always relaxed and happy and never demanding anything from me. With the age difference, there was no sexual tension at all that I could tell. We were just two colleagues, friends and parents hanging out together.

"What do you want to watch?" Sune asked with the remote in his hand.

I yawned. "I don't care, just something relaxing. What's on?"

"Some American series. 'Desperate Housewives' is probably the best I can do."

I yawned again. "I don't care much for shows like that. Anything else?"

"An old Danish movie."

"That's more my dad's thing."

"A crime magazine."

"Too real."

"The news."

"Way too real. I've been avoiding the world the last couple of days. I'm not working until tomorrow."

We ended up on some documentary that I never quite figured out. My concentration was interrupted when my phone rang.

I picked it up. I didn't recognize the number.

"Yes?"

"Rebekka Franck?"

"That's me."

"My name is Caroline Gyldenlove."

I sat up at once in the sofa and signaled Sune to turn off the TV.

"Yes."

"I don't know if you remember me. We met when you interviewed my father."

She talked with a distinguished voice, and that made her sound much older than her twenty years.

"I remember you very well. You were with your father at the Riding Club in Klampenborg."

"Mattssons. Yes. That's where my father and I go for a ride every now and then. We like it there because it is so close to the park."

"What can I do for you?"

"I am terribly sorry to disturb you and your family at this late hour, but I am concerned about my father."

"Why? What happened?"

"I don't know where he went..."

"But?"

"But he seemed so out of it."

"Is that unusual for him?" I asked, remembering the sadness I detected when I walked with him in Dyrehaven.

"No, it's not. He's always carrying the sorrows of the world on his shoulders. A big sadness. But today he seemed different. Like something had changed him."

"How is that?"

"Like he had made a decision. He was so decisive."

"Is that a bad thing? Why would you worry about that?"

"I don't know, maybe it's silly. But he looked at me before he left and said the oddest thing."

"What?"

"He said he would leave now, and if he never came back, he wanted me to know that his company, the cars, the house, everything in his name, was mine, and that I would have enough money to get everything I needed or wanted in this world."

"Why would he say that?"

"I don't know. At first, I didn't think much about it, but now I'm wondering about it. What if something is wrong?"

"Why call me?"

"At first I called the police here in Klampenborg, but they couldn't do anything yet. For all they know, he'll be back in an hour or two. That's usually what happens in cases like this, they said."

"I've heard that one before," I said, and remembered how they reacted when my daughter was missing.

"So I found your number in my dad's phone from when you called him to do that interview."

"Your dad didn't take his cell phone when he left?"

"No. That's another thing I found strange. He never leaves the house without it. He's a businessman. His life is that phone."

It did sound a little odd to me. I could only come up with two reasons why he wouldn't take his phone. Either her dad had lost his mind and wandered off, or he didn't want the police to be able to track him.

"Have you any idea as to where he could have gone?"

"No."

"Did he say anything else?"

"Not that I recall."

"Anything. Just a little thing that you might think is unimportant, but might be useful to me."

"When I asked where he was going, he did say he had to finish some game."

"What were his exact words? I want you to think carefully now and give me his exact words."

"I am going to finish the game."

"A Gentleman Hunt," I murmured.

But who was the last gentleman he needed to hunt and kill? Everybody in the picture was already gone.

39

"What the hell do you want?"

Didrik Rosenfeldt Jr. stared at me with contempt in his eyes. Sune and I had found his apartment at the port of Copenhagen, in one of the most expensive apartment buildings in the country. The complex was white as snow, and all the apartments had views of the ocean and Sweden in the horizon.

Didrik wasn't alone in the apartment. I heard a woman shouting from inside. She came to the door and stood behind Didrik. She was only in her underwear and stockings, but that didn't seem to bother her. Probably not his wife, I thought.

It was a long shot, I knew that, but by now, he was the only one who might know where Ulrik Gyldenlove went to meet his last victim. That was why we were there.

But right now he didn't quite seem to be willing to help us.

"Well, come on; I'm in the middle of something here. Tell me, why are you here? Have you come to ask me to fuck off again?"

I smiled. "I actually don't have time for that. But we need your help," I said.

"My help?" Didrik snorted. "To do what?"

"I would rather not discuss it out here. Can we please come in for a second?"

That obviously wasn't quite his plan for the evening, so he hesitated for a moment before he let us in.

The view was spectacular. The penthouse apartment had an ocean view from every room. On the other side of the water, I could see moving lights from cars driving along the coast of Sweden and on the bridge connecting the two Scandinavian countries.

"So what is it that is so important that it can't wait until the morning?" Didrik said.

First, I told him everything about our investigation and then the call from Ulrik Gyldenlove's daughter.

"It's urgent that we find him," I said.

After my explanation, Didrik no longer had that same smirk on his face that he'd had earlier. Luckily, he seemed to take me seriously.

"Could it be himself that he's going to kill?" he asked.

"You mean he's gone to commit suicide? I had the same thought when his daughter told me about the phone," I said. "I thought he was the last person in the picture still alive and he couldn't go on living."

"But no matter what, it's important to find him," Sune said.

"Yes, we need to stop him," I said.

Didrik nodded pensively.

"But why do you think I can help you?"

"We don't know. It was a wild shot. But maybe you know of some place your father and his friends used to meet, or a special place they talked about. Something. Anything."

He nodded again. "I might know where he could have gone."

40

The door to the school gymnasium at Herlufsholm Boarding school was locked when we arrived an hour later. It was dark and there was no light anywhere except from the lamps outside the dorms. The gymnasium was in a secluded building a distance from the main buildings of the school.

Didrik Rosenfeldt Jr. had told me that his father and his friends used to meet there at night. They would smoke cigarettes in the boys bathing area and they would climb the ropes and beat each other up for fun on the gym mats.

This was their place to hang out.

The school itself was secluded in a forest, far away from everything, and the young boys never had anywhere else to go. Didrik Rosenfeldt Jr. explained he had been a student at the school too.

Now, Sune and I stood outside the main door to the gymnasium, trying to find a way in. We had seen a car parked in the grass not far from the building, and now I spotted another expensive-looking one in the parking lot. Maybe a Jaguar or a Mercedes. The one on the grass was an old and ordinary Toyota.

"There's no one here," Sune said.

"I'm not so sure." I pointed at the expensive car in the parking lot.

"That could belong to one of the teachers at the school."

"Wouldn't that teacher park the car near the school entrance then? It's a pretty cold night."

Sune nodded. "You might be right."

"If the boarding school boys used to meet in the gymnasium, they probably wouldn't have used the main entrance where they could be seen," I said.

"Probably not. They risked getting kicked out of school if they went outside after lights out."

I nodded. That was what Didrik Rosenfeldt Jr. had told us.

"So, what you are saying," Sune continued, "is that there must be another way in."

"Exactly."

I started walking around the building when Sune stopped me.

"We don't need that," Sune then said.

I looked at him with surprise.

"What do you mean?"

He took out a screwdriver from his jacket pocket.

"I learned a lot in juvenile prison that every once in a while comes in handy." He started working on the door.

I was impressed. Less than a minute later, the door was open.

We went in. It was totally dark and we couldn't see anything. But, as we moved forward, I suddenly heard voices. Two men were talking. They were standing on a platform at the end of the gym. Face to face but with distance between them. Sune and I moved closer and soon we could see them. I had a hard time recognizing their faces in the darkness. But I knew their voices.

"Thank you for your call," one said.

I recognized the voice as the one of Ulrik Gyldenlove.

"The last time we saw each other, Zenia was still alive," the other one said. Everything inside of me froze. I knew that voice. It belonged to Michael Oestergaard, the detective at Karrebaeksminde Police Department. Michael, I thought. Michael Clausen. He must have changed his name. Of course. Bjorn Clausen's younger brother. The one who married Zenia Petersen when she got pregnant after the rape.

"It was at that party," Ulrik said. "At the school. Here in this gymnasium. The band was playing on this stage, remember?"

"You and your friends were graduating. I was a sophomore. The whole school was at that party," Michael said.

"It was 1986." Ulrik sighed. "Seems like forever ago."

"And yet still so diabolically haunting and crystal clear in our memories," Michael said.

"She danced with me right here on the floor," Ulrik said, while he pointed. "So young, so beautiful."

"So alive," Michael said.

Ulrik nodded.

"She might have been dancing with you, but she was looking at me while she was in your arms," Michael continued.

"I remember that very well. That made me so furious."

"And that's when you and your friends decided I needed to be taught a lesson, right? I was, after all, only a sophomore."

"So was Zenia."

"Yes, but she was a girl. A very pretty one too. And popular among the seniors. Especially you. And no one messes with a senior's girl, right?"

"That was the hierarchy. That's just the way things were."

I heard Ulrik sigh deeply and then he sat down on a chair with his head bowed. Michael took a step in his direction. His voice was filled with anger and hate when he opened his mouth again.

"You made me watch it."

Ulrik hid his face in his hands.

Michael continued, "You beasts made me watch while you...raped her."

Ulrik looked up. "I can still sometimes hear her screams at night," he said.

"So can I. I tried to help her. But Bjorn held me back. I couldn't move, no matter how much I fought."

"The endless remorse I have felt over the years can never wipe out the torment Zenia must have carried," Ulrik said.

He looked up at Michael, who was now standing right in front of him.

"Do what you have to do," Ulrik said.

In the faint light, I saw Michael Oestergaard raise his hand with the claw. I stepped forward.

"Tell me, when you cut through the chest of your victims, is it enough to just do it once, or do you need to do it several times before he dies?" I asked.

Sune had found a light switch and turned it on.

The two men looked at me.

"What a strange question," Michael Oestergaard said.

"Just trying to make conversation."

"I don't have time for your games," he said, and lifted the hand with the claws high up in the air.

"Just do it," Ulrik said.

Sune stood right behind me. I tried not to show it, but I was really scared. What if I didn't stop him in time? Would he kill him? Would he kill us afterwards?

"Is this what you think Zenia would have wanted?" I asked, in another attempt to buy us some time. Sune had called the police and they would be here any moment.

The claw came down to his side. I took in a deep breath and tried to calm myself. He was talking to me now. If I could only stall him for a few more minutes.

"They made me watch them as they…" he said with hatred spitting out of him. "I couldn't do anything. Bjorn was holding me."

"He always was the strongest one," Ulrik said.

"That must have been horrific," I said.

"They even held my eyelids open with their fingers so I would see everything. And I did. She looked me right in the eye while Ulrik did it to her. He was on top of her back, holding her hair, riding her like a horse, while Henrik and Bertel held her arms and legs. She looked me straight in the eyes. And I was helpless. After that, she had nothing left to live for. She couldn't bear to see her own child. She didn't know who the father was. And then she killed herself...and him. Now I have nothing left. After she died, I tried everything to forget her. I even changed my last name to my mother's maiden name. I got into the police force, but nothing ever replaced her. So, one day, I decided to start planning my revenge."

"What's with the claw?"

"My brother had it. I found it when we cleared out his room after he died. He made it for them back then. He was a farm boy like me, remember. We both knew how to make stuff like that on my dad's welder."

"So that was where he made the glove and that's where you made the cross to put through Bertel Due-Lauritzen's skull?" I asked.

He nodded and then continued.

"My brother and his friends used to take the glove when they raped girls on their boat. It was Didrik who was fascinated by horror movies, my brother had told me. One of them would dress up like Freddy Krueger and scare their victims by singing the song and threatening to kill them with the claws. I thought it would be the ultimate way to get my revenge by using their own glove."

"What happened to your brother?"

"I found out a short time later that it had all been his idea. When he was with Didrik, he became an animal. He wanted to impress him and be like him. He enjoyed seeing me suffer that night. He liked holding me, he told me. So I killed him six months after his graduation. I had to. I couldn't stand looking at him anymore. It was so easy. I knocked him down and pushed him over the bridge so he landed on the tracks. Then I waited for the train to do the rest. After that, I thought I had gotten my revenge, but a few years later, Zenia killed herself, and then there was no turning back. I had to kill them all."

"But would Zenia want you to do this? Is this the solution?" I asked.

"At least it will finally all be over. She was all I had. They destroyed her. I loved her and I even loved the child. I thought of him as mine. And now they're both gone."

"Do it. Just do it!" Ulrik ordered.

Michael looked at him, then lifted the claw again. My heart pounded. How could I stop him? I heard sirens outside. It was only a matter of seconds.

"Don't do it. It won't bring Zenia or your child back," I tried one last time, but no one was listening to me anymore. It was all between the two men and their past.

They were no longer sensing anyone else. They didn't care. It was time to finish what they had started. And they would do it here where it all began.

"I'm the last one. Everybody else is gone. Just do what you have to do," Ulrik continued. He stood up in front of Michael.

"Nine, ten, you will never sleep again..." Michael sang, as he swung the hand with the metal claw and it went straight into Ulrik's chest, causing him to tumble onto the floor.

"No!" I screamed.

Less than one second later, the building was filled with uniforms and guns, pointing at everybody and everything. I put my hands in the air to signal I was unarmed, and Sune did the same. Then I saw two policemen throw Michael onto the floor.

Ulrik was still lying motionless on the stage floor.

41

A week later I was on my way to Enoe. I drove, thinking about the last couple of weeks and how crazy it had all been. Ironically, I had wanted to come here to get a quieter life for my daughter and myself. Meanwhile, we had the first serial killer on the loose in the history of our small country, and my daughter had been abducted by her own father, who had almost killed her with sleeping pills.

Wow! It had been a crazy couple of weeks.

Michael Oestergaard was now in police custody and would get his punishment. Under interrogation, he had admitted that he was the one who trashed my dad's place. A detective had told my father that Michael wanted to scare me after he had seen me in Christian Junge-Larsen's apartment.

The media was all over it, but I had been the one to break the story. It was mine. It was a solo. And my editor had loved every step of it.

Luckily, Ulrik Gyldenlove had survived. His daughter said he was in pretty bad shape, but he was going to survive. I don't quite know who would consider it lucky. I would, and his daughter would, but he probably wouldn't. He wanted to die. He went to the gymnasium to die that night.

The case was closed and that had a nice feeling to it. I had done my part to solve it, and now the rest was in the hands of the police. The only thing I couldn't quite figure out on my own was why the pastor had tried to find Zenia Petersen. The answer came by itself. I talked to Irene, who explained to me that she got a visit from him a few years ago when he just began ministering. He wanted to apologize for what they had done. Since he now was a pastor, he said, he needed to repent for the past.

He had even called my sister too. She told me later when I told her everything. She and I had gotten closer after this. She had called me several times and invited me to dinner at her house and told me to bring Dad too. So the whole story seemed to have done some good. For me at least.

Sune had gotten an apology from the police and had then taken a week's vacation with Tobias and left for a cabin in Sweden. They would be back next week and we would be on to new adventures. My daughter was looking forward to seeing much more of her new best friend in the future.

Now I only had one thing left that needed to be put back in order.

He greeted me in the driveway, barefooted, as always. I drove up to the beach house and got out of the car. I looked at him and smiled.

"I am sorry," I said.

Giovanni took my head in his big hands and lifted it up. Then he kissed me.

When he was done, I laughed.

"What is so funny?"

"At one point, I actually thought you were the killer."

He didn't laugh, but looked at me seriously.

"Really? Why?"

Me and my big mouth I thought. Now I had offended him.

"Because you have spikes and a welder, and one of the victims was killed by two spikes that were welded into a cross."

Now he was laughing. I was relieved.

"I am a sculptor. I make sculptures out of stone or iron by welding it. I use spikes to cut the stone."

He put his arm around my neck and we walked into his beach house. The ocean was calm outside.

"So you really thought I could kill someone?" he asked, when I had a glass of red wine in my hand.

I smiled. "Well, you fit the profile of a true psychopath," I said, and kissed him while we both laughed out loud.

THE END
  Want to know what happens next?
  Get the sequel in the Rebekka Franck series here :
  Three, four ... Better lock your door

AFTERWORD

Dear reader,

Thank you for purchasing *One, Two ... He is coming for you* (Rebekka Frank #1).

I hope you enjoyed reading it as much as I did writing it. I have released the first three books in a new mystery series that you might like. The main character, Jack Ryder, is a single dad, detective and an avid surfer. It takes place in Cocoa Beach in Florida. You can read an excerpt from it on the following pages.

Jack Ryder even has his own Facebook page. Follow him here: https://www.facebook.com/Jack Ryder

You can get Hit the Road Jack and my other books and series below.

Take care,
Willow Rose

Connect with Willow online and you will be the first to know about new releases and bargains from Willow Rose
Sign up to the VIP email here:

http://readerlinks.com/l/415254
I promise not to share your email with anyone else, and I won't clutter your inbox. I'll only contact you when a new book is out or when I have a special bargain/free eBook.

Tired of too many emails? Text the word: "willowrose" to 31996 to sign up to Willow's VIP text List to get a text alert with news about New Releases, Giveaways, Bargains and Free books from Willow.

ABOUT THE AUTHOR

 The Queen of Scream aka Willow Rose is a #1 Amazon Best-selling Author and an Amazon ALL-star Author of more than 80 novels. She writes Mystery, Paranormal, Romance, Suspense, Horror, Supernatural thrillers, and Fantasy.

Willow's books are fast-paced, nail-biting page-turners with twists you won't see coming.

Several of her books have reached the Kindle top 20 of ALL books in the US, UK, and Canada.

She has sold more than six million books all over the world.

Willow lives on Florida's Space Coast with her husband and two daughters. When she is not writing or reading, you will find her surfing and watch the dolphins play in the waves of the Atlantic Ocean.

Cover design by Juan Villar Padron,
https://juanjjpadron.wixsite.com/juanpadron

Special thanks to my editor Janell Parque
http://janellparque.blogspot.com/

CPSIA information can be obtained
at www.ICGtesting.com
Printed in the USA
BVHW030557100321
602114BV00001B/102